ANGELA CARTER

The Passion of New Eve

W0006733

CW00953636

BLOOMSBURY
CLASSICS

First published 1977 by Gollancz
This edition published 1993
Copyright © 1977 by Angela Carter

Bloomsbury Publishing Ltd, 2 Soho Square,
London W1V 5DE

A CIP catalogue record for this
book is available from the British Library

ISBN 0 7475 1587 5

10 9 8 7 6 5 4 3 2 1

Jacket designed by Jeff Fisher
Typeset in Great Britain by Hewer Text, Edinburgh
Printed in Great Britain by St Edmundsbury Press, Suffolk

One

The last night I spent in London, I took some girl or other to the movies and, through her mediation, I paid you a little tribute of spermatozoa, Tristessa.

A late show, a crowded cinema. The drunks all stubbornly remained unmoved and jeered, laughed and catcalled throughout your film though sibilantly hushed by pairs of sentimental queers who, hand in hand, had come to pay homage to the one woman in the world who most perfectly expressed a particular pain they felt as deeply as, more deeply than, any woman, a pain whose nature I could not then define although it was the very essence of your magic. The film stock was old and scratched, as if the desolating passage of time were made visible in the rain upon the screen, audible in the worn stuttering of the sound track, yet these erosions of temporality only enhanced your luminous presence since they made it all the more forlorn, the more precarious your specious triumph over time. For you were just as beautiful as you had been twenty years before, would always be so beautiful as long as celluloid remained in complicity with the phenomenon of persistence of vision; but that triumph would die of duration in the end, and the surfaces that preserved your appearance were already wearing away.

But oh, how beautiful she had been and was, Tristessa de St Ange, billed (do you remember?) as "The most beautiful woman in the world", who executed her symbolic autobiography in arabesques of kitsch and hyperbole yet transcended the rhetoric of vulgarity by exemplifying it with a heroic lack of compromise.

I think it was Rilke who so lamented the inadequacy of our symbolism – regretted so bitterly we cannot, unlike the (was it?) Ancient Greeks, find adequate external symbols for the life within us – yes, that's the quotation. But, no. He was wrong. Our external symbols must always express the life within us with absolute precision; how could they do otherwise, since that life has generated them? Therefore we must not blame our poor symbols if they take forms that seem trivial to us, or absurd, for the symbols themselves have no control over their own fleshly manifestations, however paltry they may be; the nature of our life alone has determined their forms.

A critique of these symbols is a critique of our lives.

Tristessa. Enigma. Illusion. Woman? Ah!

And all you signified was false! Your existence was only notional; you were a piece of pure mystification, Tristessa. Nevertheless, as beautiful as only things that don't exist can be, most haunting of paradoxes, that recipe for perennial dissatisfaction.

Both memory and prescience were at work in me when I and a girl whose name I don't remember went to see Tristessa in *Wuthering Heights* the last night I was ever in London.

Tristessa had long since joined Billie Holliday and Judy Garland in the queenly pantheon of women who expose their scars with pride, pointing to their emblematic despair just as a medieval saint points to the wounds of his martyrdom, and no drag-artiste felt his repertoire complete without a personation of her magic and passionate sorrow. Her stills became posters; she inspired a style for one season, they named a discotheque after her, and a chain of boutiques. But I myself had loved Tristessa out of pure innocence when I was a little boy and the sculptural flare of her nostrils haunted my pubescent dreams. The wall of my cubicle at school had been plated with her photographs. I even wrote to MGM and received, in return for my ink-stained, ill-spelt love-letter, a still from *The Fall of the House of Usher*, she, ethereal in her shroud, just risen from her coffin to the manner born.

But also, unexpectedly, quite unsolicited by me, they sent me a shot of her in trousers and sweater, swinging, of all things, a golf club. A long, lean, flat-chested woman in an attitude of posed spontaneity who showed her teeth in a grin that did not come naturally to her, for when she was in sole charge of issuing her rare smiles, they came in a code that signified nothing to do with joy. I was shocked and bewildered by this photograph. This photograph marked the beginning of my disillusion with Tristessa.

And, just at that time, she herself began to go out of fashion for, however hard they tried to force her into the mould, she had nothing whatever in common with the girl next door. There had been a baleful vogue for romanticism in the late forties; when it flickered out, health and efficiency became the motto. Strong-women with bulging pectorals were the new stars; bread, rather than dreams. Body, all body, to hell with the soul. MGM's publicity department sent me this photograph to show Tristessa was only human, a girl like any other girl, since they had lost confidence in the mythology they had created for her. The "princess lointaine" now, must learn to ride a bicycle and so forth. But Tristessa could make only the most perfunctory gestures towards real life, even if her life depended on it. And, besides, nobody had ever loved her for anything as commonplace as humanity; her allure had lain in the tragic and absurd heroism with which she had denied real life.

Tristessa, the very type of romantic dissolution, necrophilia incarnate, pretending to be a *sportswoman*? Although both photographs were signed, "loving you always, Tristessa de St A," in a strange, spiky hand, I did not bother to pin either of them up on my wall, for the one outfaced the other . . . how could I ever envisage Madeline Usher playing golf? I'd dreamed of meeting Tristessa, she stark naked, tied, perhaps to a tree in a midnight forest under the wheeling stars. To have encountered her on a suburban golf-course? Or Dido in the laundromat. Or Desdemona at the ante-natal clinic. Never!

She had been the dream itself made flesh though the flesh I knew her in was not flesh itself but only a moving picture of flesh, real but not substantial.

I only loved her because she was not of this world and now I was disillusioned with her when I discovered she could stoop to a pretence of humanity. I therefore abandoned her. I took up rugby football and fornication. Puberty stormed me. I grew up.

Still, now she was having a little camp renaissance at midnight movie festivals and she had inspired a style that spring so I took a girl whose name I forget to see Tristessa subjugate her agonised line to that of Catherine Earnshaw. For old times' sake at the cinema, I bought myself an ice-cream, since my nanny, another true fan, had taken me to watch Tristessa when I was a child and we'd always had a choc-ice apiece so that the crackle of the coat of bitter chocolate under the teeth and the sharp, sweet sting of the ice against my gums were intimately associated with my flaming, pre-adolescent heart and the twitch in my budding groin the spectacle of Tristessa's suffering always aroused in me.

For Tristessa's speciality had been suffering. Suffering was her vocation. She suffered exquisitely until suffering became demoded; then she retired to, I read somewhere, a hermit-like seclusion in Southern California, she put herself away tidily in a store-house for worn-out dreams. But by the time I read that in an abandoned magazine I picked up and flipped through on a train, I had only a retrospective, academic interest in Tristessa – I'd thought, so she's still alive, is she; she must be old as the hills.

I had a choc-ice and my companion a strawberry sundae. We sat and ate our ice-creams under the flickering blessings of the divine Tristessa. I abandoned myself to nostalgia, to the ironic appreciation of the revisited excesses of her beauty. I thought I was bidding a last goodbye to the iconography of adolescence; tomorrow, I would fly to a new place, another country, and never imagined I might find her there, waiting for revivification, for the kiss of a lover who would rouse her from her perpetual reverie, she, fleshy synthesis of the dream, both dreamed and dreamer. I never imagined, never.

When she perceived how Tristessa's crucifiction by brain fever moved me, the girl who was with me got to her knees in the dark on the dirty floor of the cinema, among the cigarette ends and empty potato crisp bags and trodden orangeade containers, and sucked me off. My gasps were drowned by the cheers and applause of the unruly section of the audience as Tyrone Power, in too much hair-cream for a convincing Heathcliff, roared his grief over the cardboard moor in a torrent of studio rain.

But then I heard this otherwise forgotten girl murmur my name, "Evelyn" and to my surprise, to my furious embarrassment, I discovered she was crying for I felt her tears leak on to my knees. Crying, perhaps, to lose me, was she? How cruel I felt, when I thought that! She kept a hieroglyph of plastic in the neck of her womb, to prevent conception; the black lady never advised me on those techniques when she fitted me up with a uterus of my own, that was not part of her intention.

As far as I can remember, this girl had grey eyes and a certain air of childlike hesitancy. I always liked that particular quality in a woman for my nanny, although sentimental, had had a marked sadistic streak and I suppose I must have acquired an ambivalent attitude towards women from her. Sometimes I'd amuse myself by tying a girl to the bed before I copulated with her. Apart from that, I was perfectly normal.

A schoolteacher from New Jersey sat next to me on the plane. In her handbag she kept a card with, printed on one side, a prayer for taking off and, on the other, a prayer for landing. Her lips moved silently. She took us into the air without incident at Heathrow and prayed us down safely at Kennedy.

Then I, tender little milk-fed English lamb that I was, landed, plop! heels first in the midst of the slaughter.

Two

Nothing in my experience had prepared me for the city. American friends, colleagues, had tried to scare me with tales of muggings and mayhem but I had not believed them, not for a moment; I'd been hooked on a particular dream, all manner of old movies ran through my head when I first heard I'd got the job there – hadn't Tristessa herself conquered New York in *The Lights of Broadway* before she died of, that time, leukaemia? I imagined a clean, hard, bright city where towers reared to the sky in a paradigm of technological aspiration and all would be peopled by loquacious cab-drivers, black but beaming chambermaids and a special kind of crisp-edged girl with apple-crunching incisors and long, gleaming legs like lascivious scissors – the shadowless inhabitants of a finite and succinct city where the ghosts who haunt the cities of Europe could have found no cobweb corners to roost in. But in New York I found, instead of hard edges and clean colours, a lurid, Gothic darkness that closed over my head entirely and became my world.

The first thing I saw when I came out of the Air

Terminal was, in a shop window, an obese plaster gnome squatly perched on a plaster toadstool as it gnawed a giant plaster pie. Welcome to the country where Mouth is King, the land of comestibles! The next thing I saw were rats, black as buboes, gnawing at a heap of garbage. And the third thing was a black man running down the middle of the road as fast as he could go, screaming and clutching his throat; an unstoppable cravat, red in colour and sticky, mortal, flowed out from beneath his fingers. A burst of gunfire; he falls on his face. The rats abandon their feast and scamper towards him, squeaking.

That night, I stayed in a hotel that caught fire in the early hours of the morning – or, rather, seemed to have caught fire, for there was all the appearance of fire; dense clouds of smoke billowed out through the air-conditioning system. They promptly evacuated all the rooms. The lobby filled with firemen, policemen and disaster-loving night-walkers who drifted in through the glass doors while the roused guests in their pyjamas wandered about like somnambulists, wringing their hands. Beneath a crystal chandelier, a woman vomited into a paper bag.

And yet it seemed that nobody knew how to express panic, in spite of an overwhelming sense of catastrophe; the victims seemed estranged even from their own fear. There was a general incuriosity, almost a dazed acquiescence in disaster; though the lobby buzzed with guesses at its cause, these seemed no more nor less than conversational gambits, not attempts to define the nature of the emergency, and nobody left the building. Was it arson? Were the

blacks responsible, or the Women? The Women?
What did they mean? Seeing my stranger's bewilderment, a cop pointed out to me, inscribed on a
wall, the female circle – thus: ♀ with, inside it, a set
of bared teeth. Women are angry. Beware Women!
Goodness me!

Panic, however, seized the occupants of the hotel
eventually – but only after the all-clear was sounded,
and only then when it was broad daylight and
therefore safe to panic, as if the terrors of the night
could only be acknowledged in the day, when they
did not exist. Then the elevator, which, even in this
pricey place, was scribbled all over with the graffiti
that also decorated the walls of the lobby, filled with
wailing and expostulating men and women who had
scrambled on their clothes, seized their bags and now
checked out, white-faced and shaking. Strange.

It was July and the city shimmered and stank. I
was half-fainting with exhaustion by noon and my
shirt was sodden with sweat. I was astonished to
see so many beggars in the rank, disordered streets,
where crones and drunkards disputed with the rats
for possession of the choicest morsels of garbage.
It was hot weather the rats loved. I could not slip
down to the corner to buy a pack of cigarettes from
the kiosk without kicking aside half a dozen of the
sleek, black monsters as they came snapping round
my ankles. They would line the staircase like a
guard of honour to greet me when I came home
to the walk-up, cold-water apartment I soon rented
on the lower East Side from a young man who then
went off to India to save his soul. Before he left,

he warned me of the imminent heat-death of the universe and advised me to concern myself with spiritual matters, since time was short.

The old soldier who lived on the floor above me would shoot at the rats with his revolver; the walls of the stairway were pitted with bullet holes. Since the staircase was never cleaned, his trophies rotted there until they decomposed; he was not the man to clean them up himself.

The skies were of strange, bright, artificial colours – acid yellow, a certain bitter orange that looked as if it would taste of metal, a dreadful, sharp, pale, mineral green – lancinating shades that made the eye wince. From these unnatural skies fell rains of gelatinous matter, reeking of decay. One day, there was a rain of, I think, sulphur, that overcame in rottenness all the other stenches of the streets. That was the day a man in a stained raincoat approached me in a delicatessen as I was buying a carton of delicious mushroom and sour cream salad and assured me, in a voice of perfect, logical calm, that, on a trip to Coney Island, whilst picking his way across the crowded and excrement-littered beach, he had observed luminous wheels in the sea, which proved that God had arrived on a celestial bicycle to proclaim the last Judgement was at hand.

Groups of proselytisers roamed the streets, chanting psalms and prayers, selling a thousand conflicting salvations. The city was scribbled all over with graffiti in a hundred languages expressing a thousand griefs and lusts and furies and often I saw, in virulent dayglo red, the insignia of the angry

women, the bared teeth in the female circle. One
day, a woman in black leather trousers who wore
a red armband printed with this symbol came up
to me in the street, shook back her rug of brown
curls, reached out a strong, gnarled hand, coarsely
mouthing obscenities as she did so, handled my cock
with contemptuous dexterity, sneered at the sight of
my helpless erection, spat in my face, turned on her
booted heel and stalked scornfully away.

My dazed innocence proved, in itself, to be some
protection. When I presented myself at the university
where I had been engaged to teach, the combat-suited
blacks who mounted guard with machine-guns at
every door and window laughed uproariously at me
when they heard my cut-glass vowels and prissy
English accent and let me go. So now I had no job;
and my reason told me to scurry back, quick as I
could, to festering yet familiar London, the devil
I knew.

But: "The age of reason is over," said the old
soldier, the Czech who lived on the floor above me.
He was, God help us all, an alchemist and distilled
a demented logic in his attic in stills of his own
devising. "In this city, you will meet immortality,
evil and death," he assured me with prophetic exhilaration. His protuberant eyeballs were veined with
red like certain kinds of rare marble. He urged me to
meditate upon the virid line of the whirling universe.
He made me dark, bitter coffee and would invite me
to share his borsch and black bread in a room such as I
had never seen before, with its crucibles and alembics
and strange charts and pictures of bleeding white

birds in bottles. There was a seventeenth-century print, tinted by hand, of an hermaphrodite carrying a golden egg that exercised a curious fascination upon me, the dual form with its breasts and its cock, its calm, comprehensive face. (Coming events? . . .) I fingered his leather-bound books – the six volumes of Manget's *Bibliotheca Chemica Curiosa*, the *Splendor Solis* of Saloman Trismosin, and Michael Maier's wonderfully illustrated *Atalanta Fugiens*. The police car wailed in the street below; a loudhailer advised a number of unknown persons in an adjacent ruin to come out, since they were all surrounded. Then the sound of guns.

"Chaos, the primordial substance," said Baroslav. "Chaos, the earliest state of disorganised creation, blindly impelled towards the creation of a new order of phenomena of hidden meanings. The fructifying chaos of anteriority, the state before the beginning of the beginning."

One night, he made gold for me – yes; he did. He mixed a red powder with fifty times its own weight of mercury, added borax and nitrate and heated the mixture in a crucible. Then he stirred it with an iron rod and, hey presto! an ingot of genuine gold. He presented it to me with a flourish. He was in his sixties, I should say, with a shaggy, salt and pepper moustache stained yellow with coffee and tobacco. He had broad, slavonic cheekbones and wore a peaked cap, like a Bolshevik, when he went out into the street. He and his wife had been patriots but were betrayed. Sometimes he talked about the death camps, and how the Gestapo raped his wife, then cut her up in little pieces while he, tied to a tree in a forest clearing, watched all and could do nothing.

He made me some gold, following the same method as James Price, Fellow of the Royal Society, but I do not know if he was a charlatan, like Price, who introduced his gold into the crucible through a hollow stirring rod. But Baroslav's gold was genuine; later, I gave it to a girl named Leilah, a girl all softly black in colour – nigredo, the stage of darkness, when the material in the vessel has broken down to dead matter. Then the matter putrefies. Dissolution. Leilah.

"Chaos," said the Czech alchemist with grim relish, "embraces all opposing forms in a state of undifferentiated dissolution."

He would look out of the window at the desolation around us with unconcealed satisfaction; we must plunge into this cauldron of chaos, we must offer ourselves to night, to dark, to death. Who may not be resurrected if, first, he has not died? What intoxicating rhetoric! A vein in his forehead throbbed as though it were the motor of his brain. He was my only friend.

Why did I stay? I had no job, shortly after my interview with the occupiers they blew up the university so that was that; my apartment with the mattress on the floorboards and the well-thumbed copy of the I-Ching and the Indian hangings and the boarded-up window was scarcely an inviting home. The little money I had brought with me was quickly running out, although I never ate meat, only rice and vegetables, and spent all my evenings talking to the alchemist or else watching old movies on my absent landlord's television set. There was a little cult revival here, too, of Tristessa's films; I saw some rare ones – a curious, dark Western in which she played a nun whom the Indians pegged out on an ant-hill and left to die, and a late, ham-handed comedy in which she inadequately represented a crazy aunt. I grew used to seeing her magic face when I turned on the set after midnight – Our Lady of Dissolution was presiding over the catastrophe of the city. All was in order, even if it were the entropic order of disorder.

It was hardly an exciting life, even though it was spiked with terror; but just that terror lured me. It was my first encounter with pure terror and, just as the old alchemist assured me from the depths of his experience, terror is the most seductive of all drugs. Pervasive unease; constant fear; the shadows that pursued me through the city. Child of a moist, green, gentle island that I was, how could I resist the promise of violence, fear, madness? That the city had become nothing but a gigantic metaphor for death kept me, in my innocence, all agog in my ring-side seat. The movie ran towards its last reel. What excitement!

I knew that all about me was mined; I learned to trust nothing and nobody, not even the cop on the corner, least of all the panhandler whining for spare change as he stretched out his trembling, murderous hand. At the midnight clanging of the doorbell, the Czech sprang up from his work-bench in a passion of remembered fury, for he was a brave man; but I, more pusillanimous by far, dove deep down in my bedclothes and covered my ears with my hands in a dread which, since hitherto inexperienced, I found queasily delicious.

It was, then, an alchemical city. It was chaos, dissolution, nigredo, night. Built on a grid like the harmonious cities of the Chinese Empire, planned, like those cities, in strict accord with the dictates of a doctrine of reason, the streets had been given numbers and not names out of a respect for pure function, had been designed in clean, abstract lines, discrete blocks, geometric intersections, to avoid just those vile repositories of the past, sewers of history, that poison the lives of European cities. A city of visible reason – that had been the intention. And this city, built to a specification that precluded the notion of the Old Adam, had hence become uniquely vulnerable to that which the streamlined spires conspired to ignore, for the darkness had lain, unacknowledged, within the builders. I remembered a question from some old examination paper: "The American constitution is the bastard child of the French Enlightenment. Discuss." That we should all be happy posits, initially, a consensus on the notion of happiness. We can all be happy only in a happy world. But Old Adam's happiness is necessarily disfunctional. All Old Adam wants to do is, to kill his father and sleep with his mother. "The reintegration with the primal form," said the black goddess, opening her thighs, closing her thighs, the ramparts of darkness, upon me. Ah! But, no; we must not breathe a word of these desires in the

pure, evangelical fusion of form and function, even
if the black rats of these desires gnaw away at us
constantly, all the time eroding.

Discreetly, almost unobtrusively, at the beginning of August, the blacks began to build a wall
around Harlem, so slowly, brick by inconspicuous
brick, that hardly anybody noticed. Dreadful tales
of the exploits of their militants circulated the
lunch-counters where I ate a midday sandwich.
Lately, a revolutionary puritanism had seized them
and this defensive wall, their machine-guns, their
target practice and a fashion for rolling down Park
Avenue in tanks indicated they had taken fresh stock
of an embattled position in the ghettoes and decided
to make of it a tactical advantage. They abandoned
dandyism and narcotics; to a man, they put on
battle-dress.

As the summer grew yet more intolerable, the
Women also furthered their depredations. Female
sharp-shooters took to sniping from concealed windows at men who lingered too long in front of posters
outside blue movie theatres. They were supposed
to have infiltrated the hookers who paraded round
Times Square in their uniforms of white boots
and mini-skirts; there were rumours of a kamikaze
squad of syphilitic whores who donated spirochetal
enlightenment for free to their customers out of
dedication to the cause. They blew up wedding
shops and scoured the newspapers for marriage
announcements so that they could send brides gifts
of well-honed razors. I grew as nervous of the
menacing gleam of their leather jackets as I was of

the crazed muggers who haunted the garbage; the Women practised humiliation at random and bruised machismo takes longer to heal than a broken head.

At the end of July, the sewage system had broken down and the lavatories ceased to flush. Respectable citizens hurled the contents of freshly-purchased chamber pots into the street below out of the windows of their apartments and the bright, rich smell of shit added a final discord to the cacophony of the city's multiple odours. The rats grew fat as piglets and vicious as hyenas.

One day of late August, when the leaves of the trees in Washington Square were touched with the first glint of poignant gold, I saw a team of plump and energetic rats the size of six month babies hurl themselves on a German shepherd, as at the sound of an unheard-by-me whistle, before the eyes of the dog's owner, a well-preserved, bottle blonde woman in her early forties who helplessly dabbed at the air and twittered while the rats tore all the flesh off the dog in three minutes and reduced him to a glittering skeleton, although the Czech alchemist, whom I had persuaded out for a promenade and a sandwich, peppered them with a hail of bullets from his pocket pistol.

On the way home, I slipped into a supermarket. It had no windows, now, because the plate glass had been smashed so often they bricked up the places where the panes had been. I bought a carton of milk. There were more armed guards than customers parading the gondolas. The Czech stayed outside to glance at the headlines on a news-stand.

When I emerged from the brisk chill of the air-conditioning, I found he had been beaten to death in my absence, although the blood and hair on his empty pistol indicated this hero of the resistance had furiously laid about him with the butt before the unknowns vanquished him. Now I was quite alone in the city. His will left instructions he should be cremated, along with the contents of his laboratory; I attended to all his wishes with a European fidelity. As soon as his body was removed to a mortuary and I had cleared out the crucibles and alembics, they let his apartment to a topless, bottomless go-go dancer named Mitzi but her tenancy did not affect me at all for, the very night of Baroslav's funeral, I met the girl who called herself Leilah and, after that, I spent most of my time with her.

The profane essence of the death of cities, the beautiful garbage eater. Her sex palpitated under my fingers like a wet, terrified cat yet she was voracious, insatiable, though coldly so, as if driven by a drier, more cerebral need than a sexual one, as if forced to the act again and again by, perhaps, an exacerbated, never-to-be-satisfied curiosity. And, almost, a vindictiveness – yet a vindictiveness directed towards herself, as though, each time she submitted herself, not to me, but to a craving she despised, or else to a loathed but imperiously demanding ritual, as if this, this exorcism by sensuality, was what her sensuality needed to make it real.

She was black as the source of shadow and her skin was matt, lustreless and far too soft, so that she seemed to melt in my embraces. Her voice was

shrill and high and would swoop up and down an
octave in a sentence or an expostulation; her speech
contained more expostulations than sentences for she
rarely had the patience or the energy to put together
subject, verb, object and extension in an ordered and
logical fashion, so sometimes she sounded more like
a demented bird than a woman, warbling arias of
invocation or demand.

I was lost the moment that I saw her.

I went to the drugstore at midnight to buy
cigarettes. The drugstore was on the corner of
the block and so I risked it for it was only a
little way away and, since my poor friend was
dead, I was reckless from grief. She was flicking
over the magazines, humming a soft tune to herself
as she did so. Her tense and resilient legs attracted
my attention first for they seemed to quiver with
the energy repressed in their repose, like the legs of
racehorses in the stable, but the black mesh stockings
she wore designated their length and slenderness as
specifically erotic, she would not use them to run
away with. As soon as I saw her legs, I imagined
them coiled or clasped around my neck.

She had on a pair of black, patent leather shoes
with straps around the ankles, fetishistic heels six
inches high and, in all the heat and paranoia of
summer, an immense coat of red fox was slung
around her shoulders; I will always associate her,
with some reason, with foxes. This coat revealed
only the hem of a dark blue, white coin-dotted dress
that hardly covered her. Her hair was a furze-bush,
à la Africain, and she had bright purple lipstick

on her mouth. She loitered among the confession
magazines, chewing a stick of candy – a Baby Ruth,
or some other item of edible Americana, singing a
soft, high, vacant, lonely song. There was a drugged
smile on her face.

In the midnight drugstore, the bored guard sat on a
plastic stool and thwacked his nightstick idly against
his thigh. The air-conditioning hummed. Outside,
traffic passed. I bought my Luckies, unzipped the
package and lit up; the trembling of my hands made
my flaring match quiver.

As soon as I saw her, I was determined to have her.
She must have known I was staring at her, a woman
always knows, though she never once glanced in my
direction, but a certain quivering, as of the antennae
of her extravagant hair, suggested she was aware of
every nuance in the atmosphere around her that she
charged with the electric glamour of her presence as
she moved away from the rack of papers, sucking
at her candy and singing an indecipherable lyric in
a dazed, almost incoherent way in that very high,
very childlike voice.

My cock was already throbbing before, at the
door, she turned towards me and let her coat fall
back. I saw her dress was a sleeveless, vestigial
shirt-waist and she had unbuttoned the front to flaunt
small, high, pointed breasts on which the nipples,
painted bright purple to match her mouth, stuck out
a full half-inch from the flesh. Her white, rolling eyes
caught mine and stared at me for an endless second
with all manner of mocking invitations in their
opaque regard. Then she extended one hand, with

the shards of five purple beetles glittering on the tips of the fingers, drew the bosom of the dress together and, with a magnificent, barbaric, swirling gesture, wrapped the coat again entirely around her, so she seemed a fully furred creature, a little fox pretending to be a siren, a witching fox in a dark wood. She was entirely the creature of this undergrowth. The door swung to and fro behind her. She was gone.

The bored guard registered her departure.

"Whore," he said; nothing could alleviate his ennui. He took a piece of well-chewed gum from his mouth and stuck it beneath his stool as I darted through the still-swinging glass door after her.

Most of the streetlamps on this block had been shot out but those that were left were of the soft, pink colour that the city authorities had hoped would reduce the aggression of the inhabitants. These lights cast a cosmetic and indulgent glow over the depredations that took place beneath them. A wasted, inner-city moon to which pollution lent a mauvish tinge leaked a few weak beams upon my prey as she swayed on shoes so high they took her a little way out of this world; they transformed her into a strange, bird-like creature, plumed with furs, not a flying thing, nor a running thing, nor a creeping thing, not flesh nor fowl, some in-between thing, hovering high above the ground which was, all the same, its reluctant habitat.

I could hear her wordless song above the inter-mittent roar of the traffic, although she sang so very softly; yet her voice was so high it seemed to operate at a different frequency from the sounds of the everyday world and it penetrated my brain like a fine wire. She wandered down the vile street, picking her way among the refuse with the rapt delight of a shepherdess in a pastoral straying among flowers in a meadow. I caught the sharp reek of musk from the furs that swung about her shoulders with a vivid life of their own, as if they were accompanying her, not as if she possessed them.

Her recklessness, to saunter, singing so, so brilliantly decorated, up and down the desperate streets, appalled and enchanted me; it was infectious, I caught it. Under the dying moon, she lead me on an invisible string through back streets where winos and junkies lay among rubble and excrement. Her vague song, now loud, now soft, her lascivious totter that sometimes broke into a stumbling dance for a few seconds, the hot, animal perfume she exuded – all these were the palpable manifestations of seduction.

Yet she seemed to manufacture about herself an inviolable space. In a parking lot, out of the corner of my eye, I saw three men stamping on the prone body of a fourth; she, too, must have seen it for she let forth a ripple of laughter that sounded like the windbells at the window of my apartment, this blythe, callous, ghetto nymph. But, when she glimpsed a rape, she moaned and scurried on for a while. So she led me deep into the geometric labyrinth of the heart of the city, into an arid world of ruins and abandoned construction sites, the megalopolitan heart that did not beat any more. The yellow taxis with their armoured windows roared by and the rats congregated in twittering battalions around the hamburger stands. The shadows were harsh, unkind.

But such was the pentacle in which she walked that nobody seemed able to see her but I and, as if I, too, had become part of her miracle, I walked unmolested, also, although the dark pageant of the night unrolled around me in its usual fashion.

She knew that I was following her for she often cast a liquid glance over her shoulder and, now and then, softly laughed. But there was a strange, magic space between us; when I was so close to her the smell of musk almost overpowered me, she would gather her coat about her and hurry a little and, though she did not seem to move fast, she must have moved far more quickly than I for I could never catch up with her. And I thought, if she were not wearing such heavy shoes, she would surely be flying; her shoes are all that anchor her to the ground. They are in complicity with gravity but she is not.

We reached an intersection and she crossed to the road island and left me stranded on the kerb behind her because the lights had changed: DON'T WALK. That was when she first overtly acknowledged my presence. She turned towards me, laughing, and her face changed as if supercharged by pure merriment. Punctuated as she was by the passing trucks and cars, I saw her open her coat to show me, once more, two nipples like neon violets; then the sign exhorted me: WALK. When I reached the island, she had fled already but my feet tangled in the snare she left for me, a twist of dark cotton spotted with white. It was her dress. I could scarcely breathe.

I picked it up and wiped my sweating forehead with it.

She stood idly, gazing vacantly between the bars of the iron grille that covered a window of a shop that sold toiletries, but when I reached the place where she had stood, she was already half a block away. The streets of night were deserted of other walkers; only evil doers waited in doorways. A dreadful innocence protected her. She was like a mermaid, an isolated creature that lives in fulfilment of its own senses; she lured me on, she was the lorelei of the gleaming river of traffic with its million, brilliant eyes that intermittently flowed between us.

Once, when she was perhaps fifty yards away from me, under the lighted portico of a movie theatre that showed a revival of *Emma Bovary*, outlined against the face of Tristessa, a face as tall as she was, she halted, as if suddenly purposeful, and disappeared for a moment behind a red-painted pillar on which had been inscribed that fearful female sign. When she emerged, she let drop some black, wispy thing and, as I now ran towards her openly welcoming smile, she became, as if miraculously translated, as if all the time no more than trick photography, posed against a Coke stand fifty yards further ahead, placidly drinking a bright pink milk-shake and laughing, with a great display of yellow, brown-streaked teeth.

So I reached the thing she had dropped and picked it up. I knew what it was before I handled it, though I could not believe it, even when I held it, her – I noticed – crotchless knickers. I buried my face in the sexual black nylon and the lace felt as healthily abrasive against my lips as her pubic hair would do. Around us, as if cut out of dark paper and stuck against the sky, were the negative perspectives of the skyscrapers. She set down her empty goblet with its spent striations of artificial cream and now she was off again, my marsh-fire, and I stumbled after her as fast as my erection, which was now gigantic, would permit me.

We came to a place where the rats outnumbered humanity five to one. Now we were in a dismal zone of crumbling tenements and, though this zone was not alive, nevertheless it was peopled. The rusting fire-escapes that wound round and round the buildings carried a freight of folk who had not been able to sleep in the heat and the humidity and now, in night attire or underclothes, had come out to try to catch whatever breath of freshness or coolness might ripple through the brazen air of the waning middle of the night. They sat upon the iron rungs of the fire-escapes in attitudes of intense silence and immobility, so deeply were they absorbed in the pursuit of refreshment, for the air was like a sewer and it took the utmost concentration and a continuous, highly disciplined effort of will to obtain any life from it.

We had walked for hours, for miles.

In the doorway of a dingy apartment block under a pathetic single bulb that still shone over the step, she turned to me again and, as I approached, let fall her bright fur so she stood quite naked but for her stockings, the scarlet garters that held them up and the spike-heeled shoes that now she bent, with an infinite display of erotic guile, to unfasten. As if perfectly unconscious of me, she rolled the mesh stocking down one black, matt thigh, upon which the coarse mesh had left indentations as tragic as if the flesh had been pressed against barbed wire in an attempt at an escape from a prison camp in which she had always lived, would always attempt to flee, would always fail.

Before she could pull off the stocking, I was upon her. I took hold of her roughly and pressed the most intransigent part of myself against her, under the mean light of the bulb, in the street of ruinous tenements where the silent, blind-eyed residents imbibed the foul air that turned them all to stone. She showed no surprise at all at my embrace but laughed and wriggled away from me, subtle as a fish.

From one hand swung her shoes, that would have made a painful weapon; and, once she'd felled me with a heel, she could have strangled me with her garters. For a moment, I knew how defenceless I was, how much at risk; above the pounding of my blood, I could hear the high-pitched conversations of the rats in the hall beyond the gaping doorway and see the shadows that converged there. The darkness inside terrified me.

But, in the grip of such savage desire, I was unable to sustain fear as fear. I only felt it as an intensification of the desire that ravaged me. She drew away from me and put one finger on her lips, gesturing me to silence; with her free hand, she took hold of mine, she drew me – she impelled me.

For one moment, one moment only, just before she touched me, just as she touched me with the enamelled blades of her fingertips, just as I crossed the filthy threshold of that gaunt, lightless, vertical, extinguished apartment block, all tenanted by strangers, my senses were eclipsed in absolute panic. This panic bore no relation to any of the titillating fears I had, up to that moment, experienced in the city; it was an archaic, atavistic panic before original darkness and silence, before the mystery of herself she unequivocally offered me, a mystery that also had its penetrable equivalence in this house with its many, many rooms, all tenanted by strangers. And, scrawled in chalk upon the wall, one piece of graffiti that could have perturbed me if I'd rummaged the meaning of it out of my memory: INTROITE ET HIC DII SUNT, a tag, the incomprehensible nudged at the edges of my mind . . .

I felt all the ghastly attraction of the fall. Like a man upon a precipice, irresistibly lured by gravity, I succumbed at once. I took the quickest way down, I plunged. I could not resist the impulsion of vertigo.

Little red fires, the eyes of rats, darted away from us in the hallway as she drew me by her small, cold hand up the spiralling staircase, up, up, up, until we came to her room where roaches swarmed on the floor and the worm-eaten night-light of the city flooded in through a curtainless window. The door slammed behind us. She dropped her shoes with a dull thud on the splintered floorboards. I kissed her. Her mouth had a strange flavour, like that of those mysterious fruits, such as the medlar, that are not fit to eat until they are rotten; her tongue was incandescent.

She dropped her fur on the floor, I stripped, both our breathing was clamorous. All my existence was now gone away into my tumescence; I was nothing but cock and I dropped down upon her like, I suppose, a bird of prey, although my prey, throughout the pursuit, had played the hunter. My full-fleshed and voracious beak tore open the poisoned wound of love between her thighs, suddenly, suddenly. Leilah, the night's gift to me, the city's gift.

How do you earn a living, Leilah? She was a naked model, she said, and sometimes she danced, naked, or else decorated with bows and tassles; and sometimes she took part in a simulated sex-show as, perhaps, the filling in a chocolate sandwich or a layer in a mocha layer cake. So she earned enough for her rent; she did not eat much, anyway. Who had given her her fox-fur coat? She stole it, she said, with a burst of tinkling laughter. And she was seventeen; and her mother, she said, was somewhere in California.

And why me, Leilah, why me? Why did you choose to give yourself to me in such a rococo fashion? But she giggled and would not reply to that.

She made me instant coffee on a grease-caked electric hot-plate, there was artificial cream made from corn-syrup solids to go with it. She flung up the window to let the smell of sex out and then we had to shout at one another over the roar of the traffic, awakened with the dawn. Her argot or patois was infinitely strange to me, I could hardly understand a word she said but I was mad for her and threw myself upon her several more times in the course of the morning although she herself showed no signs of satisfaction, only of yearning, of greater and greater irritated yearning. By lunchtime, the dark lipstick on her nipples had been transferred completely to my own pale flesh. I must have impregnated her either the very first night or else that foetid forenoon, I suppose.

What did she do all day when she wasn't working? She lay in her narrow, iron bed of white-painted iron the landlord must have stolen from a hospital, ate hash candy she made herself, so much hash candy her teeth were rotting, and dreamily agitated her clitoris with her forefinger, her mind – as far as I could tell – full of diffuse, purplish and crimson shapes that came together and divided in patterns that, as she described them to me, seemed singularly listless, limp, exhausted, as though her dreams were wearier by far than she was. When she remembered to switch it on, she would play, over and over again, the same record of a soul singer or a Motown group on a very expensive stereo system. Sometimes, when she remembered to do so, she would change the record and then the new one, too, would play over and over again, over and over and over again. Where did you get the record player, Leilah?

At the free store, she said and laughed; she meant the sound system, it, too, was stolen. She popped a lump of hash candy in my mouth. She was unnatural,

she was irresponsible. Duplicity gleamed in her eyes
and her self seemed to come and go in her body,
fretful, wilful, she a visitor in her own flesh. Her
skin was like the inside of a glove. I licked her all
over and pulled her down upon me; the crucible of
chaos delivered her to me for my pleasure, for my
bane, and so I gave her Baroslav's gold.

In the curtainless, carpetless room, with torn
pictures of soul singers on the wall, she danced
her naked dance for me and for her reflection in
her cracked mirror. She was black as my shadow
and I made her lie on her back and parted her legs
like a doctor in order to examine more closely the
exquisite negative of her sex. Sometimes, when I
was exhausted and she was not, still riven by her
carnal curiosity, she would clamber on top of me
in the middle of the night, the darkness in the
room made flesh, and thrust my limp cock inside
herself, twittering away as she did so like a distracted
canary, while I came to life in my sleep. Waking just
before she tore the orgasm from me, I would, in my
astonishment, remember the myth of the succubus,
the devils in female form who come by night to
seduce the saints. Then, to punish her for scaring
me so, I would tie her to the iron bed with my
belt. I always left her feet free, so she could kick
away the rats.

Then I would go out and leave her to her
punishment. I wandered through the disordered
streets, I, now, in full possession of Leilah's sweet,
blurred, safe world of early childhood, every day
a day of promise, of surmise, for I was eating as

much of her hash candy as she did. I would come
home in the evening with a box of fried chicken
pieces or a sack of hamburgers; she had never
made the least effort to free herself. She would
be lying just as I had left her, her brackish eyes
fixed – if "fixed" be not altogether too taut and
positive a description of their wandering gaze –
upon the ceiling. But sometimes, in revenge, she
would have fouled the bed.

If she had fouled the bed, I would untie her and
use my belt to beat her. And she would foul the bed
again, or bite my hand. So these games perpetrated
themselves and grew, I suppose, more vicious by
almost imperceptible degrees. She seemed to me a
born victim and, if she submitted to the beatings
and the degradations with a curious, ironic laugh
that no longer tinkled – for I'd beaten the wind-bells
out of her, I'd done *that* much – then isn't irony the
victim's only weapon?

I used to adore to watch her dressing herself in
the evenings, before she went out to the clubs, the
theatres, the restaurants where she performed, which
I never visited. I would lie on her bed like a pasha,
smoking, watching, in her cracked mirror, the transformation of the grubby little bud who slumbered all
day in her filth; she was a night-blooming flower.
But, unlike a flower, she did not grow beautiful by
a simple process of becoming. Her beauty was an
accession. She arrived at it by a conscious effort.
She became absorbed in the contemplation of the
figure in the mirror but she did not seem to me
to apprehend the person in the mirror as, in any

degree, herself. The reflected Leilah had a concrete form and, although this form was perfectly tangible, we all knew, all three of us in the room, it was another Leilah. Leilah invoked this formal other with a gravity and ritual that recalled witchcraft; she brought into being a Leilah who lived only in the not-world of the mirror and then became her own reflection.

These preparations extended over some hours. To decorate the other was her sole preoccupation at these times; she did not hear me if I spoke to her. When at last she assumed the darkly luminous appearance of Lily-in-the-mirror, she became her; everyday Leilah disappeared immediately. My Leilah was now wholly the other one. She turned to kiss me quickly, with an absent-minded dignity that she only acquired through the mirror; the mirror bestowed a grace upon her, now she was her own mistress.

And then she tripped off on her tall shoes to some benighted cabaret.

Regular as clockwork, once a night she witched me, night after night. Oh, my domestic brothel! All the delights of the flesh available in one institution of bone and muscle. The finicking care she used to give to the creation of this edifice! Applying the rouge to her nether lips and the purple or peony or scarlet grease to her mouth and nipples; powders and unguents all the colours of the rainbow went on to the skin in the sockets of her eyes; with the manual dexterity of an assembler of precision instruments, she glued on the fringe of false eyelashes. The topiary of her hair she would sometimes thread with beads

or dust with glinting bronze powder she also applied
to her pubic mound. Then she sprayed herself with
dark perfumes that enhanced rather than concealed
the lingering odour of sexuality that was her own
perfume. What would the poor scrubwoman back
home in the ghetto of Watts say if she could see you
now, Leilah, Lilith, mud Lily, as you slip on another
pair of the sequinned knickers that function as no
more than a decorative and inadequate parenthesis
round your sex?

So she ingeniously put together this seductive
apparatus while Joe Tex or Al Green played on
the stereo.

Her dresses were rags of chiffon or of slimy,
synthetic fabrics or harsh-textured, knitted, metallic
stuff – gold and silver and copper. Her stockings
were made of black, or purple, or scarlet mesh;
her vertiginous shoes combinations of shiny leathers
dyed green, pink, purple or orange. She walked in
technicolor. Sometimes she put on eccentric boots
that laced up to her knee but left her toes bare.
Sometimes she lashed her calves with thongs, like
a slave. Then, bedizened like Rahab the Harlot but
armoured with an impregnable plating of corrupt
innocence, she would fling yet another fur – for she
possessed a tea chest full of furs, even a chinchilla
stole – she would fling a scarf or cloak or jacket of the
beautiful pelts of animals around the extraordinary
sloping delicacy of her bare shoulders and trot off,
with the air of a good child on its way to Sunday
school, into the diabolic cleft of the night, to return
about five or six in the morning with a touch of liquor

on her breath, though never much, and a great many dollars tucked in the top of her stocking.

A great many dollars tucked in the top of her stocking. All the time I lived with Leilah, I never lacked for money. We ate well and often from the counter of the neighbourhood deli, sandwiches (pastrami on rye and so on), salami, coleslaw, fried chicken, potato salad, apple pie, blueberry pie, boisenberry pie, raspberry and redcurrant pie, peach pie, pecan pie, etc etc etc, cheesecake and strudel. We brought home egg foo-yong and wan-tun soup and fried rice in wax cartons from the Chinese restaurant and drank, I recall, a great deal of Coca-Cola from cans sweating with refrigeration.

The cracked mirror jaggedly reciprocated her bisected reflection and that of my watching self with the mauve exhalations of a joint curling round my head. To watch her dressing herself, putting on her public face, was to witness an inversion of the ritual disrobing to which she would later submit her body for, the more clothed she became, the more vivid became my memory of her nakedness and, as she watched me watching the assemblage of all the paraphernalia that only emphasised the black plush flanks and crimson slit beneath it, so she, too, seemed to abandon her self in the mirror, to abandon her self to the mirror, and allowed herself to function only as a fiction of the erotic dream into which the mirror cast me.

So, together, we entered the same reverie, the self-created, self-perpetuating, solipsistic world of the woman watching herself being watched in a mirror that seemed to have split apart under the strain of supporting her world.

Yet I have not told you what a child she was, how little, how sometimes clinging. And she had something of the awful delicacy of those china ornaments that invite you to smash them, because they are so fragile. And when she walked, she looked as though she were dancing; she had a sprightly grace that suggested how easy it would be for her to stumble, to trip, to fall.

I never knew a girl more a slave to style. It was the most important thing in the world to her that her eyelashes and the sculptured arc of her hair be just so. She did not want me to kiss her before she went out to work in case I smudge her lipstick or otherwise untidy her so, of course, so aroused was I by her ritual incarnation, the way she systematically carnalised herself and became dressed meat, that I always managed to have her somehow, at the last minute, even if it was up against the wall, while her lips stretched back to show her dark gums in an agony of affront and she gasped: "No!" and her purple fingernails scored my back more out of indignation than passion.

But soon I grew bored with her. I had enough of her, then more than enough. She became only an irritation of the flesh, an itch that must be scratched; a response, not a pleasure. The sickness ran its course and I was left only with the habit of her sensuality, an addiction of which I was half ashamed.

What she could have seen in me? She must have liked my tender pallor and my blue eyes and my

English accent she found so hard to follow, so quaint to hear. God knows what else she could have liked, except the victim's role. I gave her nothing but an ingot of alchemical gold, and a baby, and mutilation, and sterility.

She began to vomit in the mornings two or three weeks after I moved into her little room with its view of the ruins. It was growing colder. There was a chill snap to the mornings and a fine, sad mist over the Hudson. She bent over the cold water sink, straining and sobbing a little; it humiliated her to vomit in front of me. Her breasts swelled and she would not let me touch them because they hurt her so. Her period did not come. She took a sample of her urine to a clinic. Yes. She was pregnant.

How do I know it's my baby, Leilah? The oldest abuse, the most primitive evasion. Her lips skinned back and she screamed. Her eyes rolled until they were all whites. She took her case of cosmetics, flung up the sash of the window and tipped all out into the street below. She tore up her dresses and would have torn the furs but I stopped her. She ground up glass and ate it but she vomited it all up helplessly and then, weak and sick, she demanded in a hysterical falsetto that I marry her. She said it was my duty to marry her. She issued voodoo threats against my manhood; she told me a chicken would come and snap my cock off, but I did not believe that. All this witchery offended my European sensibility; it seemed to me her pregnancy had unhinged her.

As soon as I knew she was carrying my child, any remaining desire for her vanished. She became only

an embarrassment to me. She became a shocking
inconvenience to me.

Sometimes I had dragged myself out of my sensual
lethargy long enough to go back to my old apartment
on the East Side to collect my mail. I had written
to my parents that my job had fallen through and
could they, perhaps, see their way to subsidise me
sufficiently for a brief holiday, so that I could buy a
second-hand car, drive round and see something of
the States, so that my journey would not be entirely
wasted. I did not tell Leilah I had done this.

At first they prevaricated. News of the unstable
political situation in the States distressed them. They
wanted their son safe home. The blacks had burned
down Grand Central Station so there were few,
if any, commuters. The inhabitants of the inner
city had come into their own; Manhattan was an
almost medieval city, for the gutters had become
open sewers and the towers where the rich lived
were as strongly fortified as castles. There were
no lights in the street at night except those of
burning buildings. Strikes reduced utilities to nil.
The National Guard patrolled the banks; urban
guerrillas of many denominations added their bullets
to the random bullets of the streets.

But I pleaded my own adventurous spirit and told
them the European press was exaggerating the Trans-
atlantic situation to distract attention from affairs at
home, where the first National Front members had
just taken their seats in the House; there were riots
in Birmingham and Wolverhampton; the power
workers had been on strike for months. Then a

distant uncle died and left me a legacy, so they could not make any excuses about money. Now I received a banker's order from them for a sufficient amount, even at the present price of gasoline. I had planned a luxurious itinerary in my head, during those purple hours spent between Leilah's dirty sheets . . . New Orleans, the names of whose streets were music, and all the siren South; the Spanish West; the desert . . . and now Leilah was pregnant and she seemed to see no good reason why she should not, God help me, marry me.

I told her firmly that she could not marry me and she must have an abortion. She sprang at me from the bed and tried to scratch out my eyes with her poor fingernails on which the purple enamel was now pitifully chipped. But I caught her wrists easily and held her down and reminded her she was only seventeen and very beautiful, that the world must contain a great deal more for such an enchanting person as herself than a penniless young Englishman who had not even got a job. I was a perfect, sanctimonious hypocrite. Nothing was too low for me to stoop to if it meant I could get rid of her.

I capitalised on the few books and possessions I kept at the Lower East Side apartment and gave the proceeds to her. I also gave her what little of the money I had left from the sum I originally brought with me but I did not tell her about the cheque my parents had sent me since now I had set my heart on the trip and did not want to jeopardise it in any way.

And, although all I told her was true, far more true
than I wished to believe, because to acknowledge she
was indeed just as beautiful and brilliant as I told her
she was would have wounded my own vanity too
severely still, even then, I could pretend that I did
not see her contempt in the face that now shut up
all its dark petals against me.

When she came to herself, in the sullen conva-
lescence from her hysteria, she did not turn against
me. No; she became indifferent to me, though
acquiescently so. I ceased to have any significance
for her, and, in spite of myself, I was piqued. My
irresponsible vanity was a little dinted. And, in my
heart, I knew it was my own weakness, my own
exhaustion that she had, in some sense, divined and
reflected for me that had made her so attractive to
me. She was a perfect woman; like the moon, she
only gave reflected light. She had mimicked me, she
had become the thing I wanted of her, so that she
could make me love her and yet she had mimicked
me so well she had also mimicked the fatal lack in
me that meant I was not able to love her because I
myself was so unlovable.

So, hypocrites that we were, we spared ourselves
the final hypocrisy of love. Or, I saved myself
from that most brutal of all assaults, the siege of
the other.

Now Leilah became as limp, passive and obedient
as I could wish. But she trusted nobody she did not
know, so she obtained from, she told me, a girl at
one of the places where she worked the address of
an old lady from Haiti who performed abortions in

the heart of Harlem where, even if accompanied by Leilah, I myself should not venture, especially on such a mission. She herself sold a fur or two to make up the price. And the price was high, because of the magic involved. In her delirium, afterwards, it transpired this Voodoo abortionist was accustomed to sacrifice a cock before each operation and, whatever else happened, she botched the job so badly that Leilah became infected and had to go to hospital at the cost of all the rest of her furs, at the price of her womb.

I sent her off to her appointment in a cab. To give herself courage, she had dressed herself up to the nines and put on her tallest, most baroque shoes. They were of rose-pink suede, I remember, with silver heels. And her chinchilla stole. And a strip of scarlet silk disguised as a dress. She reeked of a savage perfume that was her own entirely, it did not come from any bottle. As the taxi rolled away, she threw me a backward glance. Her face seemed full of a baleful triumph, as though this extreme to which I had forced her was my own punishment and her own pain no business of hers, but all mine.

Another cab delivered her back to me eighteen hours later. She had fainted; she had suffered a massive haemorrhage. The floor of the cab was awash with blood. The driver was a black himself and, when he saw that I was not, he told me, in a voice that clanged with hatred, the lady should be taken to a clinic immediately and he held me responsible for the cost of cleaning up his vehicle.

I held her in my arms all the way. I was full of

guilt and horror yet, since the easiest way out of
my own pain at having caused her so much pain
was to cease to feel for her altogether, by the next
day, of course, I had done so. But, while the broken
thing lay in my arms with its life oozing out of its
abused femininity, I felt only that I was the cause
of all. When we drew up outside the emergency
ward, she came to life for a moment; she opened
her eyes and gave me a look of so much anguish,
I almost faltered, almost loved her. Then the heavy
lids drooped down again and I had all the forms
to sign and the money to find before they would
admit her and give her a blood transfusion.

The receptionist at the gynaecological ward treated
me with extravagant contempt. She was a sharp-
featured, scrubbed young woman with fair hair
scraped into a prim knot at the nape. Her accent
was that of an East Coast university and her eyes
were cold as chastity. She would not let me in
to see Leilah and she told me the hospital would
contact Leilah's mother, for Leilah had said she
wanted to see her mother. She told me she could
not tell me how much the bill would be, yet, but
she gave me a rough estimate. When I said that I
was very poor, she suggested I peddle my asshole
in Times Square to raise the cash. She was so cool,
so reasonable about it I could scarcely believe it and
said I would complain to the hospital authorities.
She laughed.

"What's sauce for the goose is sauce for the
gander," she said. "They tell me the first time is
the worst."

"It is her fault," I said. "She would go to Harlem, she would go to the witchdoctor."

"So what," said the receptionist and shot me down with her eyes.

The furs must be sold; and, once I had cashed my parents' cheque, I even dug into it to the extent of five hundred dollars to help poor Leilah. Then I bought a second-hand Volkswagen and packed the snub-nosed boot with a change of clothes and some food. I tried to write Leilah a letter but all that came out was rage and accusation – why did you seduce me, in the first place, if you were so innocent? Why didn't you eat pills, or get them to put a coil of plastic in your womb, or slide a disc of rubber into your hole before it swallowed me? Why did you not find yourself a clean abortionist, the city is full of them, you fool, you whore . . . and even I grew disgusted with myself when I read my own petulant whining, the only response I could muster to her catastrophe. But I ordered her some flowers, roses, red ones, and that appeased my conscience a little, since it was not a very tender one.

Only a day had passed since they admitted her. I rang the hospital from the delicatessen and the receptionist told me, very grudgingly, that Leilah, although now sterilised, would pull through and her mother was arriving that night, by air. And I could leave my money at the front desk, yes. How could a poor black scrubwoman ever afford to pay her way across the continent to visit her sick daughter, though? Perhaps an employer paid her fare out of pity, I conjectured and didn't give a second thought to Leilah's mother. No. Not a second thought.

The city had given Leilah to me and then taken her away. There was no more reason for me to stay any longer. Now random fires flickered at night where the neon had sent out its white invitations to pleasure; riot and cholera would inherit Manhattan before the snows came and there was a taste of snow already on the winds that raced up and down the thoroughfares. My brain cleared of the hashish fumes; I saw disaster clearly.

I bought potato salad and cold ham for the journey. On my way to the parked car, less than fifty yards away from it, I was set upon by young blacks, the oldest of whom could not have been more than fifteen, and severely beaten. But they did not get my money since, following the advice of the clerk at American Express, I had folded it into a small parcel, sealed it in polythene kitchen wrap in case of involuntary incontinence, and attached it in the hollow of my crotch with Scotch tape. The roar of an approaching tank scared my attackers away; I rose groggily to my feet as the conquering heroes roared past and bolted for the car as fast as my shaking legs would carry me.

So I abandoned Leilah to the dying city and took to the freeway, past flaming wrecks of cars, secure from random snipers behind my bullet-proof windows. Down the freeways in fine style, like a true American hero, my money stowed between my legs.

At first, I was exhilarated. I thought I left behind a fatal sickness that had been bred of the city; yet the darkness and confusion were as much my own as that of the city and I took the sickness with me since I was myself infected, or had brought it from the Old World to the New World with me, was myself a carrier of the germ of a universal pandemic of despair. But I wanted to blame my disease upon somebody and so I chose Leilah, for she was the nearest thing to myself I had ever met.

I said to myself: her slow, sweet flesh has suffused my own with its corrupt languor. The sickness of the ghetto and the slow delirious sickness of femininity, its passivity, its narcissism, have infected me because of her. She has been doubly degraded, through her race and through her sex; this affliction she has given me is therefore twice as virulent, I might die of it. All these absurd notions flickered through my injustice as I tore hell-for-leather through the night. As dawn came up over the New Jersey turnpike, I saw the desolation of the entire megalopolis and it was a mirror of my own.

Festering with misanthropy, dreading the pestilence I ascribed to inhabited places, I abandoned all my ill-made plans. I would not go South; there were too many ghosts of Europe in the bayous. I would go where there were no ghosts, I needed pure air and cleanness. I would go to the desert. There, the primordial light, unexhausted by eyes, would purify me.

I would go to the desert, to the waste heart of that vast country, the desert on which they turned their backs for fear it would remind them of emptiness – the desert, the arid zone, there to find, chimera of chimeras, there, in the ocean of sand, among the bleached rocks of the untenanted part of the world, I thought I might find that most elusive of all chimeras, myself.

And so, in the end, I did, although this self was a perfect stranger to me.

Three

The road. When I could drive no more for weariness I huddled in the back of the car and uneasily dreamed for a few hours but I did not do that often, I was in a frenzy that precluded rest. I felt that I was in a great hurry but I did not know I was speeding towards the very enigma I had left behind – the dark room, the mirror, the woman. I did not know this destination exercised a magnetic attraction on me. I did not know I could not stop.

In the mornings, the ground was white with hoar frost for it was now late October and a crimson sun rose over plains that rolled as far as the pale hem of the sky. There were no trees. The radio in the car fed me an aural pabulum of cheapjack heartbreak: this nasal country music was interspersed with voices that sang the praises of innumerable articles of consumption and sputtered out frequent news bulletins. The Harlem Wall grew longer, taller, thicker; the National Guard was on permanent call. Riots, incendiarism. I could not have picked a worse time for my trip. Only fatality could have possessed me to go high-tailing off in such troubled

times, fatality and the unknowable impulsion of the
destination ahead of me, a destination of which I was
entirely ignorant although it had chosen me long ago
for our destinations choose us, choose us before we
are born.

And exercise a magnetic attraction upon us, drawing us inexorably towards the source we have
forgotten. Descend lower, descend the diminishing
spirals of being that restore us to our source. Descend
lower; while the world, in time, goes forward and so
presents us with the illusion of motion, though all our
lives we move through the curvilinear galleries of the
brain towards the core of the labyrinth within us.

Nation-wide oil stocks were running low. Service
stations imposed their own rationing; prices trebled,
quadrupled, then doubled upon that. I flung down
dollars by the handful to preserve the urgency of
my flight.

I sent my parents a cable to tell them I was safe
and sound from a post office in a dusty, forsaken,
prairie village in Colorado, where the old men in
the soda-fountain shook their heads and clicked their
tongues between their teeth as they watched the
armed tussles in colour on television. The old men
in broad-brimmed hats heckled the screen in slow,
eroded voices; they would have liked the President to
bomb the blacks but did not find it imperative. It was
so much entertainment to them. They had retreated
into apartness, already; what business of theirs was
New York? Outside, in the dusty street, the wind
sang songs of loneliness in the geometric web of
power cables and telephone wires. A hamburger cost

five dollars; the meat filling would be a quarter of an inch thick, but there was still plenty of pickle.

I was possessed. I had entirely succumbed to the dementia which had seized the city. The melo-dramatic paraphernalia of history unfolding upon the television screens I glimpsed through parlour windows was of no more concern to me than the horned owls who blinked in the beam of my headlights as they perched on the roadside telephone poles. I drove day and night. Sooner than I would have believed possible, I reached the desert, the abode of enforced sterility, the dehydrated sea of infertility, the post-menopausal part of the earth.

Four

I am lost, quite lost in the middle of the desert.

I have abandoned the temperate parts of the earth. The sun burned out the eyes of the man in the service station; the dry air etched his face full of fine lines. He did not speak. That was yesterday, or the day before. The day before, or else yesterday, the wind blew my map away. The air dries out my lungs. I gasp.

There is no-one, no-one.

I am helplessly lost in the middle of the desert, without map or guide or compass. The landscape unfurls around me like an old fan that has lost all its painted silk and left only the bare, yellowed sticks of antique ivory in a world in which, since I am alive, I have no business. The earth has been scalped, flayed: it is peopled only with echoes. The world shines and glistens, reeks and swelters till its skin peels, flakes, cracks, blisters.

I have found a landscape that matches the landscape of my heart.

Five

On a road that ran through an insane landscape of pale rock, honeycombed peak upon peak in unstable, erratic structures, calcified assemblages of whiteness and silence where jostling pebbles marked the paths of rivers that dried up before time began, where snakes and lizards rustled in the grey sand, where buzzards floated in the sky, I ran out of gas and so found myself entirely at the desert's mercy. I sat in the driving seat and bravely tried to laugh at my own predicament but the echoes of my laughter sounded such a parody I soon fell silent. I had a little water in a plastic container, three halves of a ham-and-lettuce sandwich wrapped in cellophane, seventeen cigarettes and – I counted them – eleven matches. Night drew on.

With the night came a dreadful chill, as if the sun, when it dipped below the pinnacles of rock, drew with it all the heat with which, throughout the day, it had suffused the sand, leaving behind its negative, a worse-than-cold. In a little while, a sickle moon showed in a sky sparsely sewn with unfamiliar stars and I heard, a single time, in the distance, a freezing howl that made my scalp tingle. Then perfect silence.

I huddled in the back of the Volkswagen and waited for a friendly passer-by who would tow me to a township; none came. I ate one of my sandwich halves, drank a mouthful or two of water, smoked two cigarettes, the second lit from the butt of the first. I listened to the car radio until the sheer impropriety of the cheap music in this ancient and terrible place forced me to switch off. Then I tried to sleep but could not, for the desert was the most intrusive of companions.

In the first, frail moonlight, the rocks looked like weird habitations and, once or twice during the endless vigil of that night, I could have sworn I saw a light flicker here or there among the excoriated towers of the architectless town. But my eyes, and my ears, too, began to deceive me in the course of the profound silence and a darkness perhaps even more profound than the silence that dominated me as soon as the apology for a moon had set. I have spent many atrocious nights since that first night of solitude and cold, the night that introduced me to estrangement, but, since it was the first, and custom had not yet acquainted me with the peculiar horror of the desert, I don't think I've ever suffered more, no, never. I felt I was a tender grub lodged in a crack of inhospitable soil with only my little shell of thin metal, my car, to protect me. The silence stuffed my ears with fur.

I must admit I did think of poor Leilah once or twice and wondered if she were stirring and

speaking and looking at her roses but I did not
think of her often and, when I did, only with the
most gratuitous sentimentality.

The light of dawn struck a violent pallor from
the rocks. I was light-headed; I had not slept and
I was very hungry. I ate my last sandwich half,
hoarding every mouthful, as if the longer I took to
eat it, the longer it would sustain me. I moistened
my dry mouth with water and smoked one of my
two remaining cigarettes lit with my last match,
and then lit my last, final cigarette from the stub.

When I reluctantly ground it out, an idea struck
me. If I climbed to the top of a peak near the road,
I could obtain a fine view of all the surrounding
country and might be able to see, perhaps, the next
gas station – or, far away, a car approaching which
would rescue me.

I stepped out of the stale interior of the car into
the sharp, bright sunshine, I staggered at the blow
of the fresh air. Then the air split under a sharp crack
and soldered itself together, instantly. A gun shot?
Or the voiced tensions of the rocks? Or my own
ears, deceiving me? When I pulled myself together,
I picked a little way carefully among the rocks but,
before I climbed to any height, I tripped over it
before I saw it – it was a bird.

It was not yet quite dead, although a bloody
tunnel was bored into its breast feathers, feathers as tightly packed as the petals of a chrysan-
themum. In my light fever, I saw what it was at
once – the Bird of Hermes, the bleeding bird of
the iconography of the alchemists; now the great,

white, beautiful bird turns to dead and putrefying
matter. . .

It had a wing-span of perhaps six feet – angelic,
Icarian wings; but its helpless fall, precipitated by
death's bullet from its native element, had broken
and twisted the marvellous wings that had been
both sign and motor of its etherial nature. It was
enormous, as white as snow – only, the pin-feathers
were yellowish, as if tarnished.

Where had it come from? It was not a desert bird,
not an eagle or a buzzard. I did not know many names
of birds. But perhaps it was an albatross – bane of the
Ancient Mariner; ah, I knew my poetry, though. An
albatross, numinous, ominous. But what gale could
have blown it so far from the ocean to a death in the
dry navel of the desert and who shot it down, here,
where nobody was, to leave it dying on a roadside?
How ugly and pathetic the bird is, now it has been
forced to come to terms with the gravity that this
glider, this high-diver, this acrobat upon the unstable
trapeze of the heavens had spent its life defying. A
devastating sorrow overcame me when I saw the
thing that had been so beautiful so soon before
now writhe in its dishevelled extremity, such an
instantaneous metamorphosis! Its yellow eyes were
filming over.

I had some idea of digging a grave for it, I knelt
on the road and took it in my arms. It feebly beat
its wings, not yet quite gone, poor bird . . . but
a torrent of red, scavenging ants cascaded from its
eyes and wound, they'd been feasting on it, already,
before it was quite dead.

The sight of the carrion ants brought the bile into my throat. I dropped the bird, gagging. At that very moment, a brisk karate chop in the back of my neck felled me, and sent me sprawling on the ground beside the rotting albatross.

When I opened my eyes again, I went from nightmare to nightmare. I saw before me my own pale features, warped yet reflected in the black disc that covered the face of the figure who crouched above me. I closed my eyes again, in horror, but when it briskly set about going through my pockets, I started upright; it swiftly dealt me another chop and I lay low, again. When I risked a second peep, it was stowing my driver's licence, my travellers' cheques, my passport, even my dirty handkerchief into a capacious pouch it carried at its side.

Slung over its shoulder was a sub-machine-gun.

Then a bullet whizzed over my head and buried itself in the sand. My captor turned and drilled the empty air full of holes; a great, panicky squeaking rose up and, somewhere near at hand, the sound of an engine revving up. A few more bullets fell short of us and an ungainly helicopter rose into the air from the summit of the peak I'd been attempting to climb. Its propellers creaked as if it were very old, it lumbered up through the sky, roaring and groaning, and laboured away through the lucid air.

So the desert was by no means tenantless.

And I was alone with this thin, tall thing sheathed in supple garments of a leather-like substance with a jaunty, peaked cap on its head and, attached to this cap, a blank visor of black plastic that, I realised, must be a dust-shield designed for travelling in the desert, that concealed its face completely. So my superstitious terror abated a little, though not much, for it looked terribly menacing, and, although it did nothing to harm me, it did not seem any the less intimidating when I saw it wore the scarlet arm-band the Women wore.

But this arm-band did not contain a snarl within the emended female circle; instead, it carried a symbol that looked, to me, like a broken arrow or truncated column.

She had arrived on a curious little vehicle like a small jeep, with sleds instead of wheels, or sleds that could convert into wheels, obviously designed for negotiating sand, electronically powered – her arrival had made not one sound. Now she took a coil of rope from its seat and attached one end, in spite of my protests, firmly about my waist, pinning my arms to my sides. When I was securely trussed, she jumped back on her electronic sand-sled and glided off slowly enough for me to follow her at a stumbling trot – and I had no option but to do so.

Now I was a prisoner, but of whom I did not know except she was a woman.

She led me down the gully which formed a natural path through still groups of pale shadows but, when we reached a sandfield, ridged by the winds, I began to suffer terribly from the sun. I pleaded with my captress to let me rest for a moment but she might have been deaf and dumb for all the response she made; she didn't even look back over her shoulder.

The sun cruelly chastised my fair skin but she took not the slightest notice of my pleas, until at midday, when there were no shadows left, she halted, jumped down and produced a pink paper parasol from the interior of the slick, silent beast she rode in.

She unfurled the parasol and thrust the ivory handle in the sand where it cast a little, round, rosy pool of shadow in which, though she did not untie me, she invited me to sit down. She loosed one of my arms to give me back the use of it, then took a water bottle from a carrier between her handlebars but she drank deeply herself before she let me draw on it, so all I got were a few brackish mouthfuls from the bottom. She tipped up her mask to drink but I caught no more than a glimpse of her face. The water had a curious, artificial flavour.

Then she gave me a few wafers of a synthetic but not bad-tasting bread or biscuit-like substance and had some of it herself. This scientific concoction was nourishing enough, in spite of its ascetic flavour, to sustain me for the rest of the day's terrible journey, jogging along on foot over the burning sand, until, at nightfall, I arrived at the place they called Beulah.

Oh, how austere and rigorous the inhabitants of Beulah are! Beulah lies in the interior, in the inward parts of the earth, its emblem is a broken column; in Beulah, philosophy has dominion over the rocks. Mother built this underground town, she burrowed it out below the sand; Holy Mother whose fingers are scalpels excavated the concentric descending spheres of Beulah, unless, that is, she herself has always been there – a chthonic deity, a presence always present in

the shaping structure of dream. She is a holy woman,
it is a profane place.

It will become the place where I was born.

The soles of my shoes had been burned away
and my feet were raw and covered with bleeding
blisters. My one free hand, clenched on the ivory
handle of the parasol she'd kindly let me retain, was
skinned, my shirt had soaked through with sweat
and dried again and soaked again and offered me
little protection, anyway – I'd been comprehensively
grilled and so beaten about the head by the sun,
lashed by little whips of sand, my eyes so sore
and clogged with dust I could scarcely make out
the mauve transparencies of the shadows of dusk
when they invaded the sands.

The cool wind brought me no refreshment; I was
too far gone, too abandoned to the ordeal. But then
my captress halted her sand-sled, and me with it,
though I stumbled on witlessly for a few paces
since I could scarcely believe we'd come to a stop.
When I righted myself and got my breath back and
wiped the sand from my eyes, I saw she'd got out
of her driving seat and stood with arms akimbo
before a monument of carved stone that had been
erected with a grand disregard for incongruity in
the very heart of this mineral eradication of being,
in the centre of a wind-dimpled sand-meadow that
extended for acres around it.

It was a pompous structure, chipped out of granite
dragged from god knows where, it was twenty
or thirty feet tall. It cast an infinitely elongated
shadow in the direction of the night; upon a classic

pediment, it represented a stone cock with testicles, all complete, in a state of massive tumescence. But the cock was broken off clean in the middle; upon the fractured surface, a vulture with the look of a hanging judge perched and, as I thought, winked at me most horribly. The top half of the cock, ten feet of it, lay in the sand at my feet but it did not look as if it had fallen accidentally.

While I gazed in perplexity at this sculptured epitaph, my captress raised her clenched fist towards it in salute. She invited me to admire it. There was a legend inscribed on the pediment, a Latin tag: INTROITE ET HIC DII SUNT. I knew it, I'd seen it, it tugged at my memory, it reminded me of poor Leilah, though just then I'd no pity to spare for anybody but myself. Beneath this stone sits the Mother in a complicated mix of mythology and technology, which I for one will never be able to unravel though I am its inheritor; ENTER, FOR HERE THE GODS ARE.

There is a place where contrarieties are equally true.

This place is called Beulah.

At the point in time when I set eyes on that broken pillar in the heart of the desert, the thread of my life snapped in two. I'd never be, again, as I was when I'd seen it first. I'd find myself, once I'd seen it, at the mercy of a cruel and circular logic that did not operate in terms of this world.

My captress jumped back into her little sled and threw a switch. The sled darted off so quickly I pitched forward and was dragged along. As I fell,

I saw the pillar fall and the vulture flap up, startled, into the air; pillar, pediment and base fell back together, with a crash, and disclosed a yawning opening in the sand beneath them, a sloping pit that led down. Down it she drove, down a paved throat of sand into the depths of the earth. She gave me no chance to get back on my feet; she dragged me along on my face so I arrived unceremoniously in the woman's town and when, fathoms deep, I came to rest at last, I was blubbering helplessly, like a third former.

I sprawled in the sand, aware of nothing but my own abasement.

And here I am in Beulah, the place where contrarieties exist together.

Six

Descend lower. You have not reached the end of the maze, yet.

Beulah is a profane place. It is a crucible. It is the home of the woman who calls herself the Great Parricide, also glories in the title of Grand Emasculator; ecstasy their only anaesthetic, the priests of Cybele sheared off their parts to exalt her, ran bleeding, psalmodising, crazed through the streets. This woman has many names but her daughters call her Mother. Mother has made herself into an incarnated deity; she has quite transformed her flesh, she has undergone a painful metamorphosis of the entire body and become the abstraction of a natural principle. She is also a great scientist who makes extraordinary experiments and I was destined to become the subject of one of them; but I was ignorant of everything when, fainting, I arrived in Beulah.

They must have put ointment on my burns and wiped my face and eyes for, when I woke, I was no longer in much pain. I lay on a pallet on the floor of a dim, white room lit only by a fringe of

pinkish luminescence at the foot of the wall. This
room was quite round, as if it had been blown
out, like bubble gum, inflated under the earth; its
walls were of a tough, synthetic integument with an
unnatural sheen upon it that troubled me to see, it
was so slick, so lifeless. Everything in the room had
a curiously artificial quality, though nothing seemed
unreal, far from it; Beulah, since its blueprint is a state
of mind, has an unimpeachable quality of realism.
But it is a triumph of science and hardly anything
about it is natural, as if magic, there, masquerades
as surgery in order to gain credence in a secular age.
Yet now, when I think of Beulah, I am not sure I
do not exaggerate its technological marvels, either
make too much of them – or else my fallible and
shell-shocked memory has invented most of them, in
order to soften the mythic vengeance on me there.

Vengeance, I call it; though, if I've suffered
since then a clarification of the world, if now I
comprehend even a little the nature of the flesh,
I owe this knowledge to the illumination afforded
me by the sullen flash of Holy Mother's obsidian
scalpel – Evelyn, the first victim of her wild justice,
trimmed with that knife to Eve, first child of her
manufactory.

For I am not natural, you know – even though,
if you cut me, I will bleed.

The floor was flat enough, although the room
was round, and also covered with a shiny, plastic
substance. It was very cool, yet I could not hear
the hum of air-conditioning. Chill-feeling, weftless,
warpless bedcovers, a fabric that had never seen the

loom; a functional plastic neck-rest to support my still-aching head. I was so dizzy that the room, with its look of a science fiction chapel, waltzed around me, but when I saw there was no door out of this spherical place, I leapt from the bed, although I was still weak as a kitten, and began to hammer at the walls with my fists. A trap! A prisoner! Swallowed up underground and trapped! Let me out! But I could not shout loudly because the sand had got in my throat and I wheezed dreadfully, while the walls were so well insulated I made only a dull thudding on them.

Then a loudspeaker concealed somewhere in the sinister rotundities around me crackled and an unknown female voice told me I might just as well lie down again and not to waste my strength, they would come to me in their own good time. Since I saw I could do nothing, I stretched out on my mattress, again, but I could not subdue the trembling of my limbs. The voice was followed by a silence so depthlessly profound, so implacable, I knew it was the inhuman silence of the inner earth and I was far from the light of the sun.

All the fear that had been crowding in the back of my brain since I arrived in America now flooded through and through me and reduced me to stark terror. The cool, clean room with its hygienically enforced tranquillity invited me to panic because I'd grown used to disorder and now feared order as much as if it were inimical. I was utterly helpless, in a strange land, in the strangest of places – buried deep in a blind room seamless as an egg deep in a

nameless desert a long way from home. I broke
down and I think I must have called for my mother
because, when I did so, there was an explosion of
soft, ironic laughter from the concealed loudspeakers
so I knew that, however silent they were, they were
always listening to me. At that, my shame became
too much to bear and I buried my tear-stained face
in my cold bed. Oh, that low, bubbling laughter!
"Cry baby. Cry baby." No humiliation like a child's
humiliation.

Then the laughter ceased. Silence, heavy silence,
again; though my ears strained for evidence of their
breathing, I could hear nothing. When light no
longer glowed through my tight-shut eyelids, I
suspected something was up and peeked out to
find a complete darkness had arrived; the room
had been blacked out while I kept my eyes shut
and this seemed to me so sinister that I quivered
all at once with the suspicion I was about to die. I
guessed, furthermore, that my death would take the
form of an execution, though I could not imagine
what had been the nature of the crime for which, in
my absence, I'd been tried. As soon as I'd convinced
myself the girl in the black leather uniform was
going to take me out and shoot me against a wall,
the transmitter crackled again and a sonorous, dark
voice intoned: EXCEPT A MAN DIE AND BE BORN AGAIN
HE MAY NOT ENTER THE KINGDOM OF HEAVEN.

All my worst fears fulfilled!

The darkness and silence about me were as intense
as a lapse of being. We were insulated by five fathoms
of sand and rock from all natural light and sound;

yet, by degrees, the room had grown imperceptibly warmer. Now I found I was sweating profusely. Then, so gently I did not notice it at first, for at first it seemed only that the darkness changed its colour, a rosy light began to suffuse the room. The pinkish glow spread, seeped, leaked up the round walls of my cell until everything was lambent; the radiance intensified until it became reddish and, by degrees, crimson. The temperature increased until it was at blood heat. The sweat ran down me in streams.

Then the transmitter whistled and cleared. A woman's voice said: NOW YOU ARE AT THE PLACE OF BIRTH. A gong clanged, a harp or similar stringed instrument reverberated again and again. In diminishing murmurs, she assured me where I was and other women's voices took up the refrain: NOW YOU ARE AT THE PLACE OF BIRTH, NOW YOU ARE AT THE PLACE OF BIRTH . . . very softly, a lulling chorus like the distant sound of the sea. I realised the warm, red place in which I lay was a simulacrum of the womb. The voices and weird music died away; then I could hear nothing but the pounding of my own blood in my ears.

Now I felt I had been precipitated unceremoniously into the very heart of an alien cosmogony. Beneath the earth, sweating as I was in its humid viscera, I felt the dull pressure of the desert, of the mountains beyond the desert, of the vast prairies, the grazing cattle, the corn; I felt upon me the whole heaviness of that entire continent with its cities and its coinage, its mines, its foundries, its wars and its mythologies imposing itself in all its immensity, like the nightmare, upon my breast. I gasped. I choked. My fear took on a new quality; not only fear for my own safety, now, but dread of the immensity of the world about me.

Yet this specifically metaphysical dread, which shook me like a puppy shaking a rag, worrying me, destroying me, had been created with unscrupulous cunning by ingenious stage-management – a little red light, the sound of a couple of archaic musical instruments. Even my reactions were out of my own control, were strictly programmed by the tribe of desert matriarchs, the chanting women whose leather clad emissary had dragged me in such pain and humiliation over the desert.

Then the loudspeaker crackled again, to attract my attention; a gong sounded and a crisp voice with the intonations of an East Coast university delivered these maxims which, to me at that time, were quite incomprehensible.

"Proposition one: time is a man, space is a woman.

"Proposition two: time is a killer.

"Proposition three: kill time and live forever."

The gong struck again, and then the same voice delivered the following lecture.

"Oedipus wanted to live backwards. He had a sensible desire to murder his father, who dragged him from the womb in complicity with historicity. His father wanted to send little Oedipus forward on a phallic projectory (onwards and upwards!); his father taught him to live in the future, which isn't living at all, and to turn his back on the timeless eternity of interiority.

"But Oedipus botched the job. In complicity with phallocentricity, he concludes his trajectory a blind old man, wandering by the seashore in a search for reconciliation.

"But Mother won't botch the job.

"Man lives in historicity; his phallic projectory takes him onwards and upwards – but to where? Where but to the barren sea of infertility, the craters of the moon!

"Journey back, journey backwards to the source!"

A click and the transmission was over. I had not understood one word of it, though I was now very much more afraid than I had been. The matriarchs, I surmised, had captured me, and they perceived me as a criminal since they did not organise the world on the same terms as I did – the lecture, if it proved nothing else, proved that. I knew I was a criminal because I was imprisoned, although I knew of no crime which I had committed. But as soon as I defined my own status, I was a little comforted.

Then I realised I was hungry; my hunger was the only way I learned how time had passed and, somewhere outside my sealed globe, presumably, time was continuing to pass. My hunger reassured me I was still alive. I slept, in spite of my hunger.

I woke to the sound of a faint click, or chink. The room had returned to its original, innocuous, nursery pink tint and a portion of my wall had slid open; a girl, a live girl! was on the point of entering. She pushed before her a stainless steel

trolley covered with an impeccable white cloth.
The hidden contents of this trolley chinked against
one another. This girl had been my captress; I
recognised the face she had revealed when she
unmasked herself to drink from her water bottle,
but now she wore civvies, a vest or tee-shirt with,
silk-screened on the front, a design based on the
motif of the broken phallus that had greeted me
upon my arrival at the town, and a skimpy pair of
blue denim shorts. She looked, however, entirely
and comprehensively clothed, even though so much
of her skin was showing; she looked like a woman
who has never seen a mirror in all her life, not once
exposed herself to those looking glasses that betray
women into nakedness.

She did not even nod a greeting but immediately
picked up my wrist and took my pulse in an abstract,
professional manner, then thrust a thermometer in
my mouth and, while it was cooking, produced from
beneath the cloth on her trolley all the apparatus
necessary for taking my blood pressure, and forth
with did so. She nodded, the result was satisfactory;
checked the condition of the thermometer, took a
gold propelling pencil from the hip pocket of her
shorts and, with it, entered a number of hieroglyphs
on a chart attached to the trolley by a clip; then
removed the cover of a dish which proved to contain
soup, very welcome, knelt at my side and fed me
with a spoon. She administered the soup efficiently
but without kindness. It was a synthetic-tasting but
not unpalatable broth. Then she gave me some
pseudo-milk pudding, an invalid's diet.

When I had finished all the food, she stacked the plastic bowls with far too officious a clatter for the remainder of my headache and pulled back the coverlet to examine my scorched nakedness with such a cool, nurse's eye that I felt a flush of humiliation rise all over me but I was too well-grilled from the day's sunning for it to show. All this time, she said nothing at all. I had no choice but to submit myself to her. She had brought warm water with her and washed my body with a gentle enough but quite impersonal care, as though I were a corpse already. She plugged an electric razor into a wall-socket and shaved away my three or four days growth of stubble; that was the last I'd ever see of my facial hair, though I didn't know that, then.

She judiciously anointed me with antiseptic ointment which stung me so that I cried out; at that, she shot me a swift glance of such utter contempt that I bit my lip and resolved to be braver in future. She had a lean, sallow, sharp-featured face and an abrasive manner. Her tow-coloured hair was done up in two plaits. The more I looked at her, the more impossible it seemed to open a conversation with her.

After I was shaved, washed and greased, she pressed some part of the wall and it slid back to reveal a cupboard from which she produced a tee-shirt and pair of shorts just like her own. My own clothes had vanished. She dressed me. Stern as a governess, she combed out my longish, yellow hair for me, tugging at the tangles while I did a manful best not to wince. No-one had combed

my hair for years, not since my nanny, who had
indulged her spite on my elf-locks until I used to
whine and snivel. Then this girl pressed another
button and another section of the wall slid back
to show a long mirror. As I have told you, I was
slender and delicately made; now I was dressed like
this girl, I looked like this girl's sister, except that
I was far prettier than she, though not a flicker of
her eyelids registered this irony. When she saw how
startled I was at the change in my appearance, she
allowed herself a small smile. Then she took me by
the hand and the door opened again, as if by magic.
We went out into a round, narrow corridor where all
the surfaces, again, were unnatural, slippery, ersatz,
treacherous, false-looking. In Beulah, myth is a made
thing, not a found thing.

Although I could not tell which was up or which
down, or how or where to escape to, I gathered all
my little strength together and tugged away from
her but she instantly felled me with the same karate
chop she had used in the desert so I saw it was no
use trying to get free and I went quietly with her.
She spoke to me once. She said: "Oedipus was the
most fortunate man in the world, for he embraced
his fate with pleasure."

When she said that, she honoured me with the
most extraordinary smile, radiant but ambiguous,
smile of an ecstatic sphinx which changed her face
entirely, gave her a demented, maenad look.

The corridor wound round and round in descending spirals; I soon knew for certain we were bound
down. The light here was also pinkish, like an

artificial evening. We often passed the mouths of
subsidiary corridors, winding off into the depths
of the earth; these corridors were identical with
the one down which we progressed. There was a
faint, humming sound which seemed to come from
the walls themselves, a buzzy buzz that had nothing
human in it, interspersed occasionally with a metallic
twang emanating from God knows where.

It was like a trip into the labyrinths of the inner ear;
no – this was a deeper exploration, a complex system
of sequential convolutions, the linear geography of
inwardness, a tracing of the mazes of the brain
itself and I am Ariadne in the maze with this
girl's pale hand for a clue – mazes, spider-webs,
but all progressing downwards, the brain-maze of
interiority. And I was far more afraid that I'd ever
been on the pavements of Manhattan for I knew I had
unwittingly arrived at an absolute elsewhere, a place
I could never have imagined might exist, and all as
clean, as shining, as sterile as an operating theatre.
And the girl who lead me by the intransigent hand
and walked as if in possession of a virginity so
absolute no key on earth would ever be fierce or
subtle enough to try it; she was the perfect child of
the heroic sunlight and her name was Sophia. Yet
I was not too scared of her to perceive, under the
chaste rind of her tee-shirt, that she lacked a left breast
though the other was well-grown and shapely, if on
the small side. This disability softened my heart a
little towards her, although she was so very, very
cool towards me; I thought she must have suffered
surgery for cancer, and she so young, too. I did

not, then, recollect how the priestesses of Cybele
had pared away a breast and donated it to their
mother.

The walls were sealed tight upon us and it was
oppressively warm. In spite of the almost shocking
cleanness, the steely walls, the artificial light, it
seemed to me these walls must be sealed tight
upon enormous secrets. I wondered whether or not
I'd stumbled into some government establishment, a
place where they trained agents . . . had my synthetic
broth been dosed with hallucinogens? Was I being
subjected to some form of psychological testing?
I tried to hold on to these threads of reason;
yet, however hard I struggled to reconcile this
strangeness with those more familiar to me, the
synthetic apparatus of mystery that dominated this
place – its strange music, its gnomic utterances –
inexorably exerted upon me all the compulsion of
authentic mystery. In spite of myself, in spite of
the blatant spuriosity of my surroundings, they
sucked me down, crudely seduced me into a form
of belief.

Down, down, down an inscrutable series of circular, inter-twining, always descending corridors that
exerted the compulsive fascination of the mandala,
as though, in some way, I myself had made the maze
I now threaded, untenderly manacled by Sophia's
hand. My destination impelled me. The deepest
eye of this spiral drew me, beyond fear, beyond
my own unwillingness. The heavy world above us
pressed all the echoes out of our muffled footsteps,
our breathing. It grew warmer, warmer.

.Now a kind of dark curiosity began to irritate my
fear; I felt a sense of sacrilege, as if my presence here
were forbidden, and yet my captress connived at it.
I knew I was at the greatest possible risk to myself
in these convoluted passages and the spectacle that
awaited me, the Minotaur at the heart of the maze,
would be worth the price of my terror, however
high it was. So I thought, then; and my anticipation
and my fear reached a trembling peak together, for I
did not know, then, who it was that waited for me,
I did not know her awful patience, the patience of
she who'd always been waiting for me, where I'd
exiled her, down in the lowest room at the root of
my brain.

There she waited, in her eternal well-occupied
leisure, in a straight-backed chair of scrubbed pine,
the fearful, archaic thing at the core of this unnatural
helix.

She had been waiting for me all my life, I knew
it the moment that I saw her; but nothing in my
life had hinted she might always have been there,
with her menacing immobility of a Hindu statue.
One glance assured me she was sacred. She had
been human, once; and now she had made herself
into this. This!

Mother has made symbolism a concrete fact.

She is the hand-carved figurehead of her own,
self-constructed theology.

And when I saw her, I knew I had come home; yet
a desolating strangeness overwhelmed me, for I knew
I could not stay there. The great, black, self-anointed,
self-appointed prophetess, the self-created god-head

that had assumed the flesh of its own prophecy was
the destination to which her unknowing acolyte had
no option but to lead me; one woman is all women.
When Leilah lured me out of the drug-store, into
the night, towards her bed, she had organised the
conspiracy of events that involved the desert, the
dead bird, the knife, the sacrificial stone. Leilah had
lured me here, at last: Leilah had always intended
to bring me here, to the deepest cave, to this focus
of all the darkness that had always been waiting
for me in a room with just such close, red walls
within me.

For in this room lies the focus of darkness. She is
the destination of all men, the inaccessible silence,
the darkness that glides, at the last moment, always
out of reach; the door called orgasm slams in
his face, closes fast on the Nirvana of non-being
which is gone as soon as it is glimpsed. She,
this darkest one, this fleshly extinction, beyond
time, beyond imagination, always just beyond, a
little way beyond the fingertips of the spirit, the
eternally elusive quietus who will free me from
being, transform my I into the other and, in doing
so, annihilate it.

Yet there it was, in person, the mystery, enshrined
in an artificial grotto seated upon an everyday chair.
The girl Sophia kissed its forehead and gestured me
to kneel. I knelt clumsily. I was appalled by the
spectacle of the goddess. She was a sacred monster.
She was personified and self-fulfilling fertility.

Her head, with its handsome and austere mask
teetering ponderously on the bull-like pillar of her

neck, was as big and as black as Marx's head in
Highgate Cemetery; her face had the stern, demo-
cratic beauty of a figure on a pediment in the
provincial square of a people's republic and she
wore a false beard of crisp, black curls like the false
beard Queen Hatshepsut of the Two Kingdoms had
worn. She was fully clothed in obscene nakedness;
she was breasted like a sow – she possessed two
tiers of nipples, the result (Sophia would tell me,
to my squeamish horror) of a strenuous programme
of grafting, so that, in theory, she could suckle four
babies at one time. And how gigantic her limbs were!
Her ponderous feet were heavy enough to serve as
illustrations of gravity, her hands, the shape of giant
fig leaves, lay at rest on the bolsters of her knees. Her
skin, wrinkled like the skin of a black olive, rucked
like a Greek peasant's goatskin bottle, looked as rich
as though it might contain within itself the source of
a marvellous, dark, revivifying river, as if she herself
were the only oasis in this desert and her crack the
source of all the life-giving water in the world.

Her statuesque and perfect immobility implied
the willed repose of the greatest imaginable physical
strength. The sweetness of her regard implied such
wisdom that I knew, at first sight, there was no way
in which I could show her my virility that would
astonish her. Before this overwhelming woman,
the instrument that dangled from my belly was
useless. It was nothing but a decorative appendage
attached there in a spirit of frivolity by the nature
whose terrestrial representative she had, of her own
free will, become. Since I had no notion how to

approach her with it, she rendered it insignificant; I
must deal with her on her own terms. Although her
arms were the paradigm of mothering, they offered
me no refuge; that women are consolation is a man's
dream. Her fringe of breasts allowed me no place
where I could lay my head – they were not meant
for comfort, only for nourishment, and was I not
a full-grown man?

And in that belly, rich as a thousand harvests,
there was no treacherous oblivion for me for, at
birth, I'd lost all right of re-entry into the womb.
I was exiled from Nirvana forever, and, faced with
the concrete essence of woman, I was at my wit's
end how to behave. I could not imagine what giant
being might couple with her; she was a piece of pure
nature, she was earth, she was fructification.

I had reached journey's end as a man. I knew,
then, that I was among the Mothers; I experienced
the pure terror of Faust.

And she had made herself! Yes, made herself!
She was her own mythological artefact; she had
reconstructed her flesh painfully, with knives and
with needles, into a transcendental form as an
emblem, as an example, and flung a patchwork
quilt stitched from her daughters' breasts over the
cathedral of her interior, the cave within the cave.

I was at a shrine.

She spoke. Her voice was like an orchestra composed entirely of cellos, sonorosity made speech.
She invited me to sit on the floor. Trembling; I
did so.

There was a prolonged chord of savage music

followed by a chorus of women's voices uttering a stuttering, invocatory yowl: "Ma-ma-ma-ma-ma-ma-ma." Sophia turned to me and, with the aid of rhythmic intercessions of gong and harp, succinctly listed for me the aliases and properties of the goddess. At this, an aureole of golden light illuminated the object of the litany, and the chair in which she sat span slowly and hypnotically round and round, so that I saw now her huge back and great haunches, now her gigantic front, the beam of light playing over its ponderous declivities.

Ineradicable vent of being, oracular
   mouth

absolute beginning without which
   negation is impossible

in one hand she holds the sun
and the moon in the other
she shakes stars off her shoulders
when she yawns earthquakes

The moon the virgin
mother
patroness of harlots.

Danae Alphito Demeter
who reap with the sickle moon.

Ai-Uzza great goddess of Arabia Deserta

governess of the dry tides of the inward sea
  sacred stone of Mecca
tripe moon of birth of death of
  divination.

She dangles the dark key of the infernal
  regions
between her imperious fingers
Queen of the Underworld Empress of
  Demons.

Maze-queen corn-queen barley-queen
fructifier quickener pestilence-bringer
queen of the crucible.

Destiny with a terrible face
Necessity the snarler
goddess of the white wheat deliver us
  from guilt.

Our lady of the cannibals
Carridwen/Cerridwen the white sow
  pigs it in the byre.

White mare child guzzler
the meaty one.

Bare harmless children of the desert
address her in a tongue of clicks and
  grunts
Kunapipi Kalwadi Kadjara

when men put on false breasts in her
   honour.

Brigid Andaste Kekate Aateantsic
   Manat Derketo
Freija Sedna the Woman
   Rhiannon Rigantona Arianhod
Dana Bu-Ana the Good Mother
Black Anu the Cannibal

Ana or De-Ana or Ath Ana or Di-Ana
   or Ur-Ana
the heavenly one who keeps the winds
knotted up in her handkerchief.

Bellili the willow-mother
Sal-ma spring-bringer
Anna Fearina Salmana.

Governess of tides mistress of ice-fields
   mother of walruses
star of the sea
moon evening star thighs that never
   close
most immaculate of harlots.

Kali Maria Aphrodite
Jocasta.
Jocasta. Jocasta. Jocasta.

(Jocasta? Why Jocasta?) The gong emitted a final,
infinitely echoing clang, so *that* was done with.

The golden light extinguished itself; all before me simmered in a red gloom, through which those rotund and excessive forms gleamed, irrevocable as the fact of birth.

"Where is the garden of Eden?" Sophia demanded of her in a ritual fashion.

"The garden in which Adam was born lies between my thighs," responded Mother, all Mahler in her intonation, which seemed to issue from the depths of a sacred well.

She smiled at me, quite kindly.

"Because I can give life, I can accomplish miracles," she assured me.

She was so big she seemed, almost, to fill the round, red-painted, over-heated, red-lit cell in which she chose to manifest herself and I became aware of an appalling sense of claustrophobia. I'd never suffered from the condition before but now I wanted to scream, I gagged, I choked. I heard her lulling sonorities confide to me, as though revealing a great secret:

"To be a *man* is not a given condition but a continuous effort."

My knees were buckling under me, I sank lower and lower to the floor as she raised her arms and stretched them out towards me. What arms! Like girders. Like aqueducts. Her voice went down a scale of brooding tenderness.

"Don't you know you're lost in the world?"

The air was warm and crimson and pressed down upon me like a perfumed cushion, suffocating me.

"Mama lost you when you fell out of her belly.

Mama lost you years and years ago, when you were tiny."

I could not breathe; I knew I was at the place of transgression.

"Come to me, you frail little creature! Come back where you belong!"

Sophia now added an unexpectedly passionate mezzo-soprano; she adjured me with astounding conviction: "Kill your father! Sleep with your mother! Burst through all the interdictions!"

The black goddess now sways hypnotically to and fro on her throne and begins to bay like a bloodhound bitch in heat; Sophia casts off all her remaining reticence and shrieks with the enthusiasm of a crazed bacchante. There's a sudden cacophony of gongs and harps, of shrieking music. I lose my nerve in the hubbub, I whinny, mew, scrabble weakly at the sanded floor trying to burrow my way out. But Mother, possessed, cries:

"I am the wound that does not heal. I am the source of all desire. I am the fountain of the water of life. Come and possess me! Life and the myth are one!"

Her voice has its comings and goings, is blown to me as in rags on a high wind. The storm is here.

Sophia seized my trembling body as I cowered there and dragged it to the great, ululating being who now toppled from her chair to fall on her back on the floor, waving her legs in the air as fast as her girth permitted her. Her nipples leaped about like the bobbles on the fringe of an old-fashioned, red plush curtain at a french window open on a storm.

Sophia tore off my shorts with a single, ripping gesture and tumbled me onto the heaving mass of flesh on the floor.

"Reintegrate the primal form!" she urged me.

"Reintegrate the primal form!" shrieked Mother.

Her flesh seemed to me molten, burning. I caught one glimpse of her gaping vagina as I went down; it looked like the crater of a volcano on the point of eruption. Her head reared up to kiss me and, for a hallucinatory instant, I thought I saw the sun in her mouth, so that I was momentarily blinded and retain no memory of the texture of her tongue, although it seemed to me the size of a sodden bath-towel. Then her Virginia-smoked ham of a fist grasped my shrinking sex; when it went all the way in, Mother howled and so did I.

So I was unceremoniously raped; and it was the last time I performed the sexual act as a man, whatever that means, though I took very little pleasure from it. None at all, in fact, for her thighs grasped me with the vigour of the female mantis and I felt only engulfment, followed by a few seconds brisk friction. Then came a great bellow that signalled a gratification with which I myself had had very little to do and she clasped her muscles together and expelled me just as my seed pumped helplessly out and I rolled over the floor, yelping, leaving a snailtrack of gasped gobs of semen in my wake.

She rose up on her elbow and watched my exemplary humiliation with perfect impassivity.

Sophia, who had been watching us with the prim enthusiasm of a college girl at a football ballgame, now became once again a model of efficiency, produced a test-tube and a scoop from the pocket of her shorts, scraped up as much of the scattered seed as the receptacle would hold, corked it and left us alone together.

By degrees, I came to myself and Mother grew somewhat kinder, though I never realised before how degrading it is to be the object of pity. She threw me a cloth with which to wipe myself and told me to cover my private parts with it. Groaning with the weight of her own bulk as she raised it from the ground, she seated herself on her ladderbacked chair, which was of a design similar to those crafted by the godly and austere Shakers. Then she took me on her immense knee and pressed my reluctant head against her double tier of breasts. It was like being seated at the console of a gigantic cinema organ and I resented these ministrations bitterly but I could do nothing to prevent them; she was twice my size. When she spoke to me, now she laid aside the hieratic locution she adopted in her role as goddess; she grew, abstractly, tender, however condescending.

"Father doesn't know how beautiful he is. His cock intercedes with Mother for him." She slapped my balls lightly and tickled my limp helplessness with her withered black fingers, the tips of which were pinkish. "And you've abused women, Evelyn, with this delicate instrument that should have been used for nothing but pleasure. You made a weapon of it!"

And she regarded me benignly but with implicit ferocity; I stammered a little but no words came for

she was of Leilah's colour and I was full of shame.
She shrugged her immense shoulders.

"Well . . . one day, you'll discover that sexuality
is a unity manifested in different structures and it's
a hard thing, in these alienated times, to tell what
is and what is not. Ah, Evelyn, I've no quarrel with
you just because you're a man! I think your pretty
little virility is just darling, harmless as a dove, such
a delight! A lovely toy for a young girl . . . but are
you sure you get the best use of it in the shape
you are?"

What could she mean? Her face, dark as an
eclipse of the moon, is lowered over me with
giantesque solicitude; her hot, close breath basts
me, I whimper.

"Ah, don't be frightened of me, little Evelyn!"

But she held me so tightly there was nowhere to
hide my head except in her bosom and I was far
too frightened of her to do that. Mother; but too
much mother, a femaleness too vast, too gross for
my imagination to contain, a voice whose rumbling
basso-profundo set up vibrations inside my head as if
every tiny hair in the vestibule of my ear had turned
into a tuning-fork. And now my consciousness had
such huge, random gaps in it I could hardly tell
what she was doing or saying; but I think she
kissed my belly, just below my navel, I think I
remember I felt her breath tickling me and the wet
leather convulsion of her lips on my twitching skin.
And then comes the proclamation, the voice like an
army with banners:

"I see before me the fairest earth ripe for the finest

seed. In the most pure womb of Mary, there was
sown one whole grain of wheat, yet it is called a
garden of wheat –

"Hosanna! Hosanna! Hosanna!"

And all remembered sense is lost in the reverb-
erating celebrations of my annunciation, her flashing eyes, her quivering tits, and Sophia must have
thrown a switch in the hi-fi for the voice of a
vast choir with an organ and a brazen dissension
of trumpets burst apart this archetypal hole in
which I was lying with a sumptuous prodigality
of decibels.

Hosanna! Hosanna! Hosanna!

Think of the endless prairies I'm going to carve
inside you, little Evelyn. They're going to be like the
vast acreage of heaven, the meadows of eternity.

Embrace your fate, like Oedipus – but more brave
than he!

("Oedipus botched the job," they'd said; "but
Mother won't botch the job.")

And, richly, hugely, she began to bay, again; she
announced herself in thunder:

"I am the Great Parricide, I am the Castratrix
of the Phallocentric Universe, I am Mama, Mama,
Mama!"

Again, the chorus took up the hiccupping yowl,
Ma-ma-ma-ma, crashing in archaic waves over the
clamour of the trumpets and the hosannaing. And
she keeps coming and going like a trick of vision,
her voice oscillates like an audial hallucination. My
next clear memory is that now I lay on the floor at
her feet, spilled from her lap in the tumult, and she

was raising her right hand in benediction over me, although I thought I glimpsed some kind of savage irony in her smile.

"Hail, Evelyn, most fortunate of men! You're going to bring forth the Messiah of the Antithesis!"

The music slowly died away, the light ceased to simmer, clarified, and became the common light of day; but still she sat there with all her tits in double rows, the false beard, the massive negritude. She was no optical illusion, alas.

"Woman has been the antithesis in the dialectic of creation quite long enough," she opined in almost a conversational voice; I heard that quite clearly. "I'm about to make a start on the feminisation of Father Time."

A trap-door in the floor opened soundlessly and down she went into a gulf beneath, still smiling cheerfully at me. Then Sophia came, to take me away.

She had prepared me a hot bath in my cell and seasoned it with restorative powders. She was a brisk, efficient nurse but she ministered only to my body, not to my fears.

"Myth is more instructive than history, Evelyn; Mother proposes to reactivate the parthenogenesis archetype, utilising a new formula. She's going to castrate you, Evelyn, and then excavate what we call the 'fructifying female space' inside you and make you a perfect specimen of womanhood. Then, as soon as you're ready, she's going to impregnate you with your own sperm, which I collected from you after you copulated with her and took away to store in the deep freeze."

When I asked her brokenly why she should have chosen me for her mother's experiments, of what crime had I been guilty to deserve such a punishment, she answered me, with a voice like a slap in the face:

"Is it such a bad thing to become like me?"

But I was filled with consternation, stranded as I was in the middle of a nightmare in which I ate, slept, woke, had conversations and was about to suffer an operation which would transform me completely. A complete woman, yes, Sophia assured me; tits, clit, ovaries, labia major, labia minor . . . But, Sophia, does a change in the coloration of the rind alter the taste of a fruit? A change in the appearance will restructure the essence, Sophia assured me coolly. Psycho-surgery, Mother calls it. I moaned softly to myself but Sophia heard me. She was angry with me because I did not want to be turned into a woman, she rubbed me down with a towel far too harsh for my sunburn and put me to bed while heaping abuse on me but she had enough mercy to inject a sleeping drug brusquely into my arm, then left me alone. So I was forced to sleep and hoped I would wake up in the blessed Volkswagen in the desert, or in Leilah's dearly-lost bed in Manhattan, my gut convulsing with too much hash . . . but I dreamed continually of women with knives and, for some reason, of blindness; I woke, screaming, many times and always in that black egg beneath the sand, sometimes to the sound of soft laughter, but

the barbiturates were in complicity with my dreams
and drew me back into them again and again.

When Sophia came to me next, she did not bring
anything to eat, because of the operation, and she
dressed me in a stiff, white, cotton gown open down
the back. I broke down and begged her to give me
some food and show me the way out of the maze
and let me go out into the desert to take my chance
among the rattlesnakes and the vultures but she said
something I do not fully remember about time,
and mortality, and a triumph over phallocentricity,
the generator of mortality, and how the authentic
Messiah would be born of a man, had they not told
me so in school? But in my minor public school,
they had not. When I tried to hit her, she chopped
me down to the floor again with the side of her
hand. Then she tied my wrists together with rope
and so I was led, like a sacrificial animal, to the
altar, to the operating table, where Mother waited
with a knife.

Down, down, down into the dark, down into
a soft, still, warm, inter-uterine, symmetrical place
hung with curtains of crimson plush, into a curtained
cabinet where there was a white bed. A dim,
red glow, the internal light of Beulah, covered
everything. She was waiting; now she was erect,
I saw she was six and a half feet high. The lateral
repetition of the swollen ovals of her breasts looked
like row upon row of bells; she had not put on a
white coat, although she was a surgeon. There was
an overpowering sense of secrecy in that confined
place. I remember the way the curtains swished open

to reveal our audience, seated in banked seats around the little stage like the spectators of a chamber opera, rows of silent, seated women, more women than I could ever have imagined lived in this underground town – my fevered imagination thought that all the women in the world were seated there, with saucer eyes fixed upon the arena where my exemplary amputation was about to take place. Sophia untied the strings of my gown; it fell away. I was as naked as the day I was born.

And now Mother was armed. The monstrous being brandished an obsidian knife as black as she was. I found it very difficult to see, in that abattoir light, and remember, now, an atmosphere rather than an event – a lowering sense of antique ritual; of the presence, also, of stern adults who knew what was best for me better than I did myself; the full panoply of human sacrifice, in fact. Yet a perfectly twentieth-century enamelled trolley stood beside Mother, containing a covered tray which, hopefully, held syringes with anaesthetics inside them.

Sophia astonished me; she embraced and kissed me.

"You will be a new Eve, not Evelyn!" she said, with more warmth than I'd thought possible in her voice. "And the Virgin Mary, too. Be glad!"

All the assembled women clapped and cheered. Mother ran her finger up and down the blade of her knife to feel how sharp it was.

"Don't be afraid," she said in a reassuring baritone. "I'm rendering you the most fortunate affliction."

Oh, the dreadful symbolism of that knife! To be

castrated with a phallic symbol! (But what else, says Mother, could do the trick?)

I had used up all the fear within me. Now I was quite calm. Beyond despair, I surrendered myself. I had no option. It was the Dies Sanguinis, the day of voluntary castration in honour of Cybele, the scarlet ceremony of my transfiguration.

Then Sophia lifted the tray cloth and produced, to my infinite relief, a hypodermic, which she plunged into my arm. A numbing current froze my central nervous system immediately. I ceased to feel at once. But I did not lose consciousness, then. I continued to see. I lay ill at ease on the operating table and saw that dark, serrated fringe of breasts bob above me. I would have shuddered, if I could, but I was absolutely immobilised. I saw her bearded face; she smiled, half in sympathy, half in triumph.

Raising her knife, she brought it down. She cut off all my genital appendages with a single blow, caught them in her other hand and tossed them to Sophia, who slipped them into the pocket of her shorts. So she excised everything I had been and left me, instead, with a wound that would, in future, bleed once a month, at the bidding of the moon. Sophia staunched the blood with a cloth, then took another needle from the tray. This one extinguished the world completely.

And that was the end of Evelyn, who'd been sacrificed to a dark goddess of whose existence he'd never been aware – although, as it turned out, the end of the maze was yet some distance away; I'd not gone far enough, oh! by no means.

The plastic surgery that turned me into my own diminutive, Eve, the shortened form of Evelyn, this artificial changeling, the Tiresias of Southern California, took, in all, only two months to complete. During much of this time, I was deeply anaesthetised; I would, occasionally, awake to a sense of deadened pain and the knowledge of grievous internal wounds that would never heal, never. Then, as I stretched vaguely on my bed, the programming began and, wonder of wonders, old Hollywood provided me with a new set of nursery tales.

I don't know if the movies were selected on purpose, as part of the ritual attrition of my change in ontological status: this is what you've made of women! And now you yourself become what you've made . . . Certainly the films that spun out a thread of illusory reality before my dazed eyes showed me all the pain of womanhood. Tristessa, your solitude, your melancholy – Our Lady of the Sorrows, Tristessa; you came to me in seven veils of celluloid and demonstrated, in your incomparable tears, every kitsch excess of the mode of femininity.

Again and again they played me through your marvellous imitation of feeling, the whole oeuvre, from *Marguerite*, in which John Gilbert showed his profile rather too often to be an altogether convincing Faust; to the version of *Little Women* in which you made such a hash of Marmee and afterwards retired to the haunted seclusion in which I was to find you. And, to this day, I do not know if Mother wanted me to model my new womanhood upon your tenebrous deliquescence and so relegate me always to the

shadowed half being of reflected light; but now I
know that Mother knew your extraordinary secret,
I suspect some other, subtler reason. So my sickbed
was haunted by Tristessa and, on the vagarious
currents of the pain-killing drugs, I swam in and
out of your sickness, your ache of eternal longing,
your perpetual reverie, your beautiful lack of being,
as if your essence were hung up in a closet like a
dress too good to be worn and you were reduced
to going out in only your appearance.

But the psychological aspect of the psycho-surgery
did not use only Tristessa as its instrument. Now
my cell was never silent; I recall particularly three
video-tape sequences designed to assist me to adjust
to my new shape. One consisted of reproductions
of, I should think, every single Virgin and Child
that had ever been painted in the entire history of
Western European art, projected upon my curving
wall in real-life colours and blown up to larger than
life-size, accompanied by a sound track composed
of the gurgling of babies and the murmuring of
contented mothers; this was intended to glorify the
prospect before me. There was also a video-tape
intended, I think, to subliminally instil the maternal
instinct itself; it showed cats with kittens, vixens with
cubs, the mother whale with her off-spring, ocelets,
elephants, wallabies, all tumbling and suckling and
watchfully tending, furred things, feathered things,
flippered things . . . And another, more inscrutable
video-tape composed of a variety of non-phallic
imagery such as sea-anemones opening and closing; caves, with streams issuing from them; roses,

opening to admit a bee; the sea, the moon. These
visions were accompanied by the Liturgy of Holy
Mother I'd first heard Sophia recite to me the day
I'd arrived in Beulah, arranged for women's voices
in a Monteverdi-like setting, repeated over and over
again so that all the words are still engraved on my
brain. Among Mother's grander attributes, there
was a streak of inexorable vulgarity but I did not
realise its extent until I saw my new person for the
first time.

While the surgery continued in Mother's underground operating theatre in the chthonic complex
of laboratories where work went on night and
day, Sophia gave me massive injections of female
hormones daily and sometimes came and sat at my
bed-side. She would turn down the volume of the
sound of the movies and give me minatory lectures.
She was quite tender and compassionate but only as
concerned my pain; my humiliation she regarded as
a privilege. She would read me accounts of barbarous
customs such as female circumcision (had I known
how prevalent a custom it was and how it was
achieved by the excision of the clitoris?) and remind
me of how fortunate I was that Mother, by a positive
miracle of surgery, had been able to provide me
with just such a magic button of my very own.
She told me how the Ancient Chinese had crippled
their women's feet; the Jews had chained the ankles
of their women together; and the Indians ordered
widows to immolate themselves on the pyres of
their husbands and so on and so forth, hour after
hour was devoted to the relation of the horrors my

old sex had perpetrated on my new one until I would moan, in a voice that grew softer and, against my will, more musical with each day that passed, and I would try to snatch away her books with hands that continually refined and whitened themselves.

The injustice of it all left me speechless. And Sophia must know it was unjust; she knew I'd never seen the copulating snakes, the crime of Tiresias.

Unless, when I saw them, I had not recognised them.

Perhaps, I thought, they had utilised my tender body because they couldn't resist the horrid pun of my name, with all its teasing connotations. Evelyn. Why had my parents chosen to call me Evelyn, of all the names in the world? But, all the same, I twisted my head to avoid the grave censure in Sophia's eyes; her thin face reminded me of the receptionist's in the gynaecological ward, where I'd left Leilah, and this memory caused me a good deal of anguish. Sophia would sit beside me in silence, when now and then, the pain overcame the drugs' effects completely and I felt I scarcely deserved her rare, stern compassion for I guessed that somewhere, in the darkness and confusion of the city, I had transgressed and now I must be punished for it.

But, then, why should I have thought it was a punishment to be transformed into a woman?

Sophia may have been sorry to see my pain but she never pitied me because she knew I felt that I was being punished.

At the end of the second month, she took off all my remaining bandages and inspected me without a word. Then she opened the wall upon the mirror and left me alone with myself.

But when I looked in the mirror, I saw Eve; I did not see myself. I saw a young woman who, though she was I, I could in no way acknowledge as myself, for this one was only a lyrical abstraction of femininity to me, a tinted arrangement of curved lines. I touched the breasts and the mound that were not mine; I saw white hands in the mirror move, it was as though they were white gloves I had put on to conduct the unfamiliar orchestra of myself. I looked again and saw I bore a strong family resemblance to myself, although my hair had grown so long it hung down to a waist that, on the operating table, had acquired an emphatic indentation. Thanks to the plastic surgery, my eyes were now a little larger than they had been; how blue they were showed more. The cosmetic knife had provided me with a bee-stung underlip and a fat pout. I was a woman, young and desirable. I grasped my tits and pulled out the dark red nipples to see how far they'd go; they were unexpectedly elastic and it did not hurt to tug them sharply. So I got a little more courage to explore myself further and nervously slid my hand between my thighs.

But my over-taxed brain almost exploded, then, for the clitoris transplant had been an unqualified success. The tactile sensation was so well-remembered and gave me so much pleasure, still, I could scarcely believe the cleft was now my own.

Let the punishment fit the crime, whatever it had been. They had turned me into the *Playboy* centrefold. I was the object of all the unfocused desires that had ever existed in my own head. I had become my own masturbatory fantasy. And – how can I put it – the cock in my head, still, twitched at the sight of myself.

The psycho-programming had not been entirely successful.

But, where I remembered my cock, was nothing. Only a void, an insistent absence, like a noisy silence.

As I stood, naked and a stranger to myself, Mother came into the room, bringing with her a blast of the darkness under the earth. The bed groaned beneath her as she seated herself on it. She had not come to me as the goddess, today; she wore her white doctor's coat, so that I got a vague glimpse of her past self, before she transcended it – the surgeon; before that, the medical student; before that? She had brought me (Oh, God!) a dozen red roses like those I'd sent Leilah and a bunch of grapes, as if I'd just given birth to myself. I looked at these offerings with wonder. They were the first fruits of a garden I'd seen in Beulah.

"Well, Eve," she said comfortably. "How do you find yourself?"

"I don't find myself at all," I replied disconsolately.

Then her brooding eyes fixed on me with a curious sorrow, as if she feared what the future might hold for me; she trembled with the seismic contractions of her own motherliness. She beckoned me towards her, unbuttoned the front of her white coat, took

me to her breasts and suckled me. Then I felt a
great peace and a sense of reconciliation. It seemed
the breasts I suckled could never be exhausted but
would always flow with milk to nourish me and my
relation to the zone of mother had not changed and
could never change for Little Oedipus had lived in
a land of milk and kindness before his father taught
him how to stab with his phallus and baby's relation
to the breasts bears no relation to his or hers.

Now I am her daughter, am I not?

But I won't shear off a tit for her, not I!

However, in spite of my rebelliousness, which
manifested itself as early as the nipple, she managed
to comfort me a little before she told me to lie on
my back and open my legs.

She donned a headband with a small light-bulb in
the centre that shone like the third eye of a Tibetan
lama and, with its aid, peered up my new vagina
to check all was in order. She palpitated my breasts
to ascertain their structure was correct for she had
built them up to their present impressive size with
a special brew of silicone of her own invention, that
would not harden in the way Sophia assured me
the inflated tits of topless dancers did; she tested
my skin for pore-quality (superior); took my blood
pressure – why, Eve! you'll live till you're a hundred;
kissed my forehead once again, briefly, the mother;
and departed. Sophia came in and took a urine
sample.

"Don't you think," asked Sophia, "that the domi-
nation of man has caused us all too much pain? Were
you ever happy, when you were a man, since you left

the womb, unless you were trying to get back into it?" And she gave me a virgin's look of disdain.

"Will I be happy now I am a woman?" I demanded.

"Oh, no!" she said and laughed. "Of course not! Not until we all live in a happy world!"

Since your name is synonymous with wisdom, Sophia, tell me the nature of a happy world.

How will I know until I live in one?

But her face clouded over a little and she remained sunk in silent contemplation, eyeing my phial of urine as though it might contain the answer to some unspecified metaphysical problem.

When I asked Mother if I would be happy, she replied portentously: "When you were a man, you suffered mortality because you could only perpetuate yourself by proxy, through the mediation of a woman and that was often a forced mediation and hence no mediation at all. But now, first of all beings in the world, you can seed yourself and fruit yourself. With the aid of my sperm-bank, you're entirely self sufficient, Eva!

"That is why you have become New Eve, and your child will rejuvenate the world!"

Prompt on cue, trumpets and cymbals crashed off-stage; when she visited me as the goddess, clad only in her fringe of dugs, I was still overawed, and trembled. Then she spoke in rolling iambic pentameters of eternity, of the ruins of time, of psycho-sexual dynamics, and the halting of the phallocentric thrust so that the world could ripen in female space without the mortal interventions of male time. Her purple nipples would shake with the vibrations of her oratory and, even when I was most carried away by it, I would wince a little at such a gross modulation of a flesh that had once been the negative, since black, twin of my new flesh. She had been a little girl, once, quite slim and supple. And now look at her! What rage, what desperation could have forced her to mimic in her own body the refulgent form of many-breasted Artemis, another sterile goddess of fertility?

Perhaps this desert, since the nuclear tests they had performed here, somewhere in the vastness, spawned mutations of being – perpetrated hitherto unguessable modes of humanity, in which life parodied myth, or became it. And then I would shudder, the sensation, as they say, of a goose walking over my grave. But most of all, I remained bewildered.

Mother continued to peer into my interior with the aid of her headlamp every day and soon assured me the eggs in my new ovaries were ripe. They would allow me one test menstruation; they would impregnate me fourteen days after the flow ceased, the most favourable time for fertilisation.

"I'm not ready for motherhood!" I cried, in despair at my biological helplessness; but Mother and Sophia only laughed at me, if quite kindly.

I would say that, at this time, I was literally in two minds; my transformation was both perfect and imperfect. All of New Eve's experience came through two channels of sensation, her own fleshly ones and his mental ones. But at length the sense of having been Evelyn began, in spite of himself, to fade, although Eve was a creature without memory;

she was an amnesiac, a stranger in the world as she was in her own body – but it wasn't that she'd forgotten everything, no. Rather, she had nothing to remember. Nothing at all but many Virgins with many Children, a mother vixen batting its cub affectionately about the ear with a maternal paw and brownish stills from old movies, any numbers of them, ghost of a face folded in sorrow. ("Solitude and reverie," said Tristessa. "That is a woman's life.")

In the evenings, cool Sophia, who rarely modified her primness towards me, took me for walks through the galleries of sand. She showed me the plastic surgeries where a team of women had worked on my new shape according to a blue-print taken from a concensus agreement on the physical nature of an ideal woman drawn up from a protracted study of the media and constructed here, in this well-equipped studio, where Mother approved it. All the faces I might have had if I'd been a brunette or a red-head, taller or shorter or less slim in the hip were still thumb-tacked around the walls. Single-breasted women pored over drawing-boards; they'd synthesise another virgin birth as soon as they could lay their hands on another desert straggler, poor sod.

Sophia showed me the laboratories where they manufactured their synthetic milk and wafers from chemicals, spun their protein from petro-chemicals, chipped vegetable substitutes from wood. All night long, all day long, beneath the ground, these round structures hanging below the surface of the sand emitted a low, busy hum like hives of contented bees. Their energy source was the sun above us; they trapped it from the sand. Their water was their own recycled urine; Sophia escorted me through the odorous plant, past the vats of gleaming steel and sterile filters.

And all this dedicated expertise in the service of the goddess! all these women dedicated to her! For there were many, many of them, silently gliding, rarely smiling, each with but the one breast and the look in their eyes of the satisfied Calvinist who knows he has achieved grace.

Every night, at midnight, they came out of the trapdoor in the sand for their military training and as soon as she was fit to hold a gun, Eve was encouraged to join them. These exercises occupied the best part of the night and involved not only target practice and work with explosive devices, nuclear hand-weapons and limited range missiles but bayonet charges, the taking of fortified positions by assault and charges through barricades improvised from thorns and spikes. We were prepared for anything. When they marched past after these sham fights, their bodies streamed with blood and their skin hung in shreds from torn limbs. Sophia told me that Columbus and his companions had been attacked by female archers when they first set foot on the soil of the New World; Mother's asymmetric Amazons reactivated the ancient, heroic archetype, stripped like the Indians with whom John White filled his Floridian sketchbook for their drills. But Eve proved unhandy with weapons, so they laughed

at my botched shots and mocked me: "Just like
a man!"

And what was the purpose of this little army?
Would Mother's storm-troopers swoop down on
the decaying cities when my child was born of its
own virgin mother on the first day of Year One
and institute her own magic and totalitarian rule
in which time stood still and all the phallic towers
broken down? So I surmised; but nobody actually
told me so in so many words and, truth to tell, I
was so preoccupied with my own metamorphosis
I did not spare much conjecture to the question. I
knew Sophia spent what time was not consumed
in tending me by studying television newscasts in
a certain room that had maps on the walls, with
flags pinned on them; that Mother had some curious
interest in the Siege of Harlem, though I couldn't
think why . . . yet nor did I want to.

After drill was over, the Women sauntered about
in the moonlight for a breath of air and they
would chat together with great decorum; they were
perfect ladies as far as behaviour was concerned.
They treated my feelings as a former man with
a good deal of tact and consideration – far too
much, in fact; indeed, they patronised – matronised?
– me unmercifully. Their solicitous, far-too-kindly,
over-eager camaraderie, the magnanimous if teasing
way they forgave me for the graceless condition of
my former state, together with Mother's orations
and the unceasing restructuring of my personal-
ity under the twin stresses of so great a physical
change and my programming almost unbalanced

me. I felt intimations of total collapse, of absolute despair.

Sophia taught me how to make water in the way a woman does and the right way to perform one or two other biologically determined acts, how to comb my hair and plait it, to wash between my legs and under my arms and so forth but she gave me worried looks, sometimes, for I was the clumsiest of pupils – you'll have to put in more work on the programming techniques, Sophia; it takes more than identifying with Raphael's Madonna to make a real woman! And then a crippling pain like a kick in the kidneys heralded my first flow. I dabbled my finger in the bright, brown blood; I could scarcely believe it dribbled out of me but there was no way of staunching it, the source lay deep inside me, beyond my own volition, the emblem of my function. Then I knew for certain that my change was absolute and I must climb inside the skin of the girl willy nilly, whether I liked it or not, and learn, somehow, to live there.

Meanwhile, Sophia told a dreadful countdown – fourteen days, thirteen, twelve, eleven, ten – only ten more days of virginity, only nine more days until the scheduled fecundation, now only eight. I could conceive of no real existence beyond the date set for conception. I was as terrified of motherhood as any woman born. I had no plan but, in the end, desperation made me bold. The last day. Tomorrow, early in the morning, down I'd go to the operating theatre, sheeted in white . . . tomorrow!

Sophia supervised my bedtime; I still needed an

injection to make me sleep and I was not allowed
the run of the drugs cabinet for fear I'd take the
coward's way out. They were still unsure of me, but
not so suspicious as to think I'd be foolish enough to
run off into the desert without food or water, on a
little sand-sled with a battery that had only enough
juice for forty miles. . . I told Sophia I needed to
go to the communal latrines; I knew the plan of the
labyrinth now, it was like the back of my hand to
me. I darted down the mouseruns, up the smoothly
ramped corridor, past sealed-off dormitories where
the sleepy priestesses prepared themselves for bed.
The sand-sleds were kept in a parking lot directly
beneath the desert. I was in luck; somebody had just
returned from a patrol and left her vehicle carelessly
at the door to the desert – and left that door open!

I jumped into the driving seat, backed rapidly
up and out and drove away, full pelt, in the
darkness before dawn, towards the point in the
sky where I thought the sun might rise. No water,
no guide, no compass, dressed only in my regulation
shorts and tee-shirt, at that moment, as I fled the
Woman's Town, I felt myself almost a hero, almost
Evelyn, again.

Nobody came after me. Why should they? Nobody
knew I was missing; there were no alarms at the gates,
nobody wished to escape the Woman's Town, and
nobody ever came to steal from it. Only when
Sophia missed me would the hue and cry be raised
and, as I looked behind me, all I could see was the
darker shadow of the broken column sprawling on
the dark sand. I increased my speed. Sophia must have

thought I was still threading my way back through
the tunnels, or some polite sister had delayed me with
a night-cap as they often did, with their patronising
hospitality. The distance between Beulah and myself
widened; I was tearing along, the wind driving in my
face since the vehicle did not have a windscreen, I'd
forgotten to pick up one of those grim, black masks.
A dune rose like a breaker behind me and the site of
Beulah vanished. I was alone.

Even an hour alone, just then, was a blessing
to me, however brief my freedom, just that brief
freedom would be enough.

Even a brief hour of freedom and solitude, only
an hour in which I could pretend I was my old self,
again; comfort my self with the illusion I could go
home. Only an hour. . .

They knew the desert would offer me no protection, once they realised I was gone they could follow
me at their leisure, the tracks of the sand-sled would
lead them straight to their absconding Madonna
whom they would scoop up from the sand and take
back, perhaps for an extended course of surgery that
would not leave the brain intact, this time. I couldn't
hope for a remission of sentence, of course; only
for a postponement of the execution. But that was
good enough for me. And, perhaps, in my arrogant
and still unaltered heart, I remained irrationally
convinced I could escape them completely by a
sheer effort of will.

Seven

I know nothing. I am a tabula erasa, a blank sheet of paper, an unhatched egg. I have not yet become a woman, although I possess a woman's shape. Not a woman, no; both more and less than a real woman. Now I am a being as mythic and monstrous as Mother herself; but I cannot bring myself to think of that. Eve remains wilfully in the state of innocence that precedes the fall.

I had only the one thought – I'm in the most ludicrous mess in the world!

What shall I do now, if I get away from them? When I get away from them? What nursing home in all the world can right the wrong Mother has done me? I was in an abject state and, besides, I had no money; no clothes, besides the ones I wore; no passport; no means of identification; no travellers' cheques; no credit card. All my existential impedimenta had been tossed carelessly into Mother's wastepaper basket once it no longer fitted me. All that remained to me was the last thing I needed, an elaborate female apparatus, one of exquisite detail and superb charm, constructed around the nascent seed of another person, not Evelyn, whose existence, as yet, Evelyn persisted in denying. And this unfleshed other whom I was had not the slightest idea how to utilise the gadgetry of her new appearance. But how could I return to the apotheosis Mother had promised me? Impossible!

I did not know the apotheosis was inevitable and, however fast I fled, I could not run away from it but would always be running towards it. Indeed, to run away from it would be the quickest way of arriving there; my inexorable destination selects my route. I drove on.

Eight

The moon slipped over the round horizon: the headlights bored twin tunnels through the darkness before me that telescoped into themselves as I ripped down between them until at last we came to the edge of a treacherous boneyard of broken rock, one of those places where the intransigence underpinning the desert showed through. Suddenly, with an exhausted little sob, the engine cut out; no more juice. The sled slithered drearily along the sand for a few moments, with the diminishing impetus of its speed, until it stopped for good. Stranded. Now what? Keep away from them for as long as I can; any postponement of that horror is worth while. . . . I clambered out of the driving-seat; I would take cover among the rocks that might hide me for a little, for just a little longer, when the Women came after me. The sand beneath my bare feet was cold as snow but I thought I might find a cavelet where I could crouch in concealment to prolong, for however short a time, my artificial virginity and, with it, my notional unfemininity, which still remained significant to me.

As I scrambled over an outcrop, a great, black dog leaped upon me, barking furiously. It felled me to the ground and slavered at my throat. Dog, probably, of Cerberus; come to drag me back to the Underworld. God help me, I'm done for, now!

A voice gave out a sharp, yipping yell. Quick hands seized and bound me. Thin, sharp, female voices babbled discordantly above me – the Women? Women, anyway, though they spoke no language I understood. I bit their wrists and fingers and they slapped my face, to silence me. Then they dragged me over the sharp rocks to a helicopter parked in a nearby gully. That much I could see by the light of a waving flashlight – a helicopter, with its doors hanging open. I was bundled inside on to a heap of acrid-smelling cushions and pelts of animals and the girls scrambled in after me, although the dog jumped in the front seat, beside the pilot, and sat there, panting, proud as you please.

The helicopter ascended vertically from the gully while the girls, crushed together inside, hooted, roared, mewed, squeaked and clucked like a flying menagerie, in a chorus of triumph that did not contain one human word or sound. Who can they be? At whose mercy is poor Eve now? Bruised and fearful, I jolted about among them and, if one of them saw that I was moving, she would kick me.

So I was captured by Zero the poet and taken to his ranch-house in the ghost town, where they made a slave of me.

Zero the poet adored the desert because he hated humanity. He had only the one eye and that was of

an insatiable blue; he covered his empty socket with
a black patch. He was one-legged, to match, and
would poke his women with the artificial member
when the mood took him. Nevertheless, they loved
him and did not think they were fit to pick up
the crumbs from his table, at which he always
ate in solitary splendour. Sometimes, to illustrate
the humility he demanded of his wives, he would
smear his own excrement and that of the dog upon
their breasts. He stood on a rock and bayed his poetry
over the desert; once upon a time he'd written it
down but he'd grown disgusted with words and
their ineradicable human content long ago and now
all his poems were howled and danced. He attempted
to maintain an existence only in terms of expletives
and tableaux vivants; he had almost abandoned
verbalisation as a means of communication and
used everyday human speech only in circumstances
of absolute necessity, preferring for the most part a
bestial locution of grunts and barks. He loved guns
almost as much as he cherished misanthropy and
spent several hours each afternoon shooting empty
beer-cans from sticks driven into the ground on the
patio of the ranch-house.

He was the first man I met when I became a
woman.

He raped me unceremoniously in the sand in front
of his ranch-house after he dragged me from the
helicopter, while his seven wives stood round in a
circle, giggling and applauding. I was in no way
prepared for the pain; his body was an anonymous
instrument of torture, mine my own rack. My

nostrils were filled with the rank stench of his sweat
and his come and, dominating even these odours, the
sweetish, appalling smell of pig-shit, a smell which
clung to the entire ranch and its environs in a foul
miasma. When Zero had finished with me, he went
into the house with the jumping dog at his heels and
banged the door behind him. The girls picked me
up and dusted me down and took me to the room
where they ate and slept, a sorority dormitory with
Indian printed fabrics hung here and there on the
wooden walls, furnished with orange crates and lit
by flickering oil-lamps, for the electricity generator
had broken down and Zero did not have the patience
to repair it. A saddle-backed sow, caked with filth,
rose up heaving and squeaking from a mattress as
we entered the room and trampled the bare feet of
the young girls as it lurched out through the door.
Even the pigs thought they were too good for our
company.

Zero sat in solitary state in his study, the next
room. Music, Wagner, played so loudly on his
transistorised cassette recorder that it filled our
room, too.

When the girls saw I was bleeding from my
ruptured virginity, which had been no less real
because it was synthetic, one of them brought me
a bowl of cold water and a rag and they sat round
me while I cleaned myself and asked me softly,
under cover of the music, why I'd never had a
man before. I was relieved to hear they could talk
English, when they wanted, instead of the gibberish
they'd been babbling in the helicopter, but when I

started to reply in my normal speaking voice, they all vigorously mimed I should speak as quietly as they did, and their eyes moved nervously towards the door, they were afraid Zero would hear us and come storming vengefully in. For he did not allow them to speak in words. A rule they interpreted as a perpetual whispering; if Zero did not hear them, it was as if they had not spoken. All the same, they were consumed with curiosity and wanted to hear all about me and, to gratify them, I fabricated an autobiography, a cruel mother who kept me locked in the coal-shed, a lustful step-father. I took the detail from Faulkner and, when they asked me suspiciously about my accent, because it sounded strange to them, I transposed the location of these invented experiences to Canada, to account for my pronunciation. They believed everything. They were accustomed to believing everything, and, the stranger the better, the more likely they were to believe it.

They told me I was very pretty and had had a raw deal but Zero would protect me. I could see they all loved him blindly. They asked me if I were hungry; the last meal I'd eaten had been a small supper of chemical wafers at the beginning of the night so I gratefully accepted a plate filled with brown rice and puréed carrots but I had to scoop it up with my fingers because they did not have any knives, forks or spoons. In whispers, they told me how Zero believed women were fashioned of a different soul substance from men, a more primitive, animal stuff, and so did not need the paraphernalia of civilised society such as cutlery, meat, soap, shoes, etc, though, of course, he did. However, they seemed grateful to him because, out of his generosity, he allowed them the sophistication of cups and plates although these dishes were of the commonest kind and badly cracked and chipped. Their seven faces had the unused and blinded look of nuns, all postulants in the church of Zero.

They were pretty girls and I guessed that the eldest, Marijane, was no more than twenty while the youngest, Betty Louella, was only a child, perhaps twelve, perhaps less. The earnest air they shared made them look like sisters and they were dressed alike, in dungarees of faded blue denim. They were always quite naked under these dungarees. They all bore the angry marks of love-bites on the exposed flesh of throat and neck, but not one of those girls had any of their own front teeth left because Zero had sent them all to the dentist after Betty Louella once nicked his foreskin too painfully in her ecstasy whilst performing fellatio on his sacred member. They wore their hair cut very short and slashed in a straight fringe across their foreheads; each one had a wide gold wedding ring on the fourth finger of her left hand. They told me, if I were a good girl and did nothing to offend Zero, he would marry me and then there would be eight of us.

But Betty Louella's brow creased to a frown and she said, *that* would hardly be practicable because Zero's matrimonial rota was very strict and absolutely regulated their lives; indeed, I was to learn they believed it predicated their very existence, since they'd decided to believe that sexual intercourse with him guaranteed their continuing health and strength. The seven wives each spent one night of the week with Zero; the system was inflexible and never varied. Marijane as senior wife, slept with him on Sunday, Sadie on Monday and so on, with Betty Louella herself clocking in on Saturday. So there was not room in the week for a new wife. Sadie told Betty Louella not to be so silly but to trust Zero; she thought Zero would be able to attend to his eighth wife on Sunday afternoons. Sunday was a day of rest for the girls and so I would be available for my servicing after lunch.

Then Marijane exclaimed she thought *that* would be unfair because Zero might be too drained by these postprandial exertions to be able to perform his duties adequately with *her* when night fell, and what would become of her, then? She'd fade away and die, that's what she'd do – fade away like a flower that doesn't get any water, or sunshine. Then Emmeline asked, was Marijane doubting Zero's capacity? Marijane replied, no: it was out of the question to doubt Zero's capacity. Nevertheless – and here she looked at me askance, out of the corners of her eyes – since I was so pretty and new to the community, even such a stern and just man as Zero might expend too much sexual energy upon me to be able to maintain a constant supply for all . . . but Sadie made a mou of disgust and said she didn't think I was as pretty as all that. And Tiny, named for her size, opined when you got to look at me closely I wasn't really pretty at all, although I was, she supposed, all right from a distance.

Then all the rest pitched in with their opinions and soon grew heated. During the discussion, I stayed still as a statue and dumb as a stone. I was out of my depth and very nervous. After a while, Marijane, who had been looking at me all this time with increasing suspicion, said: "I guess she won't be pretty at all any more after – " and, leaving the threat hanging on the air, she seized the plate from which I'd just eaten, broke it in half and advanced on me in a menacing fashion, armed with the two, sharp, splintered surfaces. The other girls all squealed in unison, leaped up from the mattresses on which they sat and broke upon me like a wave equipped with teeth and claws. I went down under them immediately. They howled, roared and gibbered. Perhaps they were fighting for their lives. Each one seemed more desirous than the last of making her mark on my unprotected face but they were creating such a racket they disturbed Master where he sat at a leather-topped desk looted from a Hollywood producer's desert hideaway. He flung open the door between his quarters and their quarters and strode in, howling like a wolf and laying about him with a gigantic bullwhip.

The girls fell back, silenced. I crouched in the corner into which they'd driven me, whimpering. A dozen scratches scored me. Betty Louella had grazed my cheek with her broken plate, so that the flesh was raw and bleeding; Marijane had pulled out a whole lock of my hair. My flanks were gleaming with spittle, for they had spat lavishly upon me.

Zero's single eye blazed with a furious light. He shrieked as loud as he could; a huge stream of crude sound spurted directly from his anger. He seized my hand and pulled me to my feet. It must have been a Wednesday because Emmeline darted forward when he caught hold of me and began to protest it was her turn to have him that night. But he hit her with the handle of the whip and cut her lip so she sank down on her knees and moaned. We left them sullen and discontented, gazing after us with the heart-rending eyes of children denied sweeties.

Now I was alone with Zero.

He hung his whip from a nail on the bare boards of a wall on which his guns were arranged in attractive patterns, then plumped himself down on his swivelling chair of black Italian leather – for he permitted himself every luxury he could steal – and motioned me brusquely to seat myself cross-legged on the floor, which was spread with a sumptuous carpet, inch-thick and deep crimson in colour, although very dirty and fouled with dog turds. I fastidiously did as I was bid and attempted to cover myself with my abundant hair for he had already raped me once that night and I did not like the way he flagellated me with the unique lash of his regard. His dog, a lurcher, that, like its master, boasted only the one eye but balls the size of grapefruit, rose up from the luxurious basket in which it slept underneath his desk, stretched itself and approached me in order to subject me to an ordeal by sniffing. Its cold, twitching nose insinuated itself inside my navel and under my arms, so that I shivered, but when I tried to move away, Zero took up the rifle propped against his desk, clicked back the safety catch and pointed it at me. After that, I kept as still as I could and allowed the dog to nuzzle me exactly as he pleased. He called his lurcher Cain; it was the one thing Zero loved, besides the sterility of the desert.

On his desk stood a plaster bust of Nietzsche and a half-empty bottle of bourbon beside a dirty glass. The only decoration in the room, pinned to the wall behind his head, was a very large poster of Tristessa wearing the bloody nightdress of Madeline Usher. Here she was, always invariable, in this vile place – her huge eyes filled with that wild surmise, that fated quietude. Here she is, my patroness, my guardian angel: I might have known she would be here, to welcome me to pain.

But Zero had defaced her. Across this poster was scrawled, in bright red paint, the slogan: PUBLIC ENEMY NUMBER ONE and her elegiac body had been used as a target for the throwing of knives; hilts, the blades of which were embedded behind her in the wooden wall, quivered all over her. Of all the women in the world, Zero had chosen Tristessa as the prime focus of his hatred of the sex; he thought you'd bewitched him, Tristessa. He did. He truly thought so.

Zero pointed at my chest and grunted enquiringly.

"Eve," I quavered. He laughed very loudly.

"You Eve," he said. "Me Adam." But, though

he'd obviously enjoyed the jest, he seemed to resent it
had necessitated speech, his lips curled. He removed
a knife from his weapon-bristling belt, turned and
tossed it lightly at Tristessa, so that it pierced her
forehead.

"This is the lousiest lady in the world, d'you hear
me?" he announced. "She eats souls. She's magicked
the genius out of my jissom, that evil bitch! And it
won't come back until I stick my merciless finger
into this ultimate dyke, like the little Dutch boy.
Dyke; she's a dyke, a sluice of nothingness. You a
dyke?" he queried menacingly, fingering his knife.

I did not trust myself to speak, I shook my head.
He appeared to believe me, nodded, told me to
lie down on the floor regardless of the excrement
which littered it, unfastened his fly, brought out
a weapon which I now saw was of amazing size
and, with a wild cry, hurled himself upon me; he
entered me like the vandals attacking Rome. I felt a
sense of grateful detachment from this degradation;
I registered in my mind only the poignant fact of
my second rape in two hours. "Poor Eve! She's
being screwed again!" The first time he assaulted
me, I had been too overwhelmed by the horror
of it to notice what he did with his wooden leg
during intercourse; he merely let it lie beside him,
like an extra but inert member, it only came into
play during his perversions. But he was shy of it;
he would not let his women see the straps that
attached the artificial limb to his body and so he
never copulated in a state of complete nakedness but
always kept his trousers on, as Lord Byron did.

When he had finished, he rose, zipped up his leather fly and said: "Congratulations. You've just become the eighth wife of Zero the poet. You're prettier than any of them. You can have me all Sunday night. Consider the sacred fluid imparted by my member as the balm of Gilead or one true restorative. I donate you for free the elixium vitae distilled by my immaculate testicles. Alas! it won't print out any new Zeros until the Witch, the Bitch, the Dyke is dead! But not long, now, baby, not long."

In this way, I learned, to my incredulity, that this man believed the movie actress had performed a spiritual vasectomy on him. I think this was the longest that I heard him speak. Now he turned to bare his teeth venomously at the poster of Tristessa, then rooted for a moment in a drawer in his desk and produced a wedding ring exactly like the rings the rest of the harem wore. He threw this ring to me; I caught it in a cricketer's catch. My new flesh momentarily betrayed me; it swept my memory back to prep school, the smell of fresh sweat, flannel, boys' bodies, fresh cut grass . . . but it was not a real memory, it was like remembering a film I'd seen once whose performances did not concern me. Even my memories no longer fitted me, they were old clothes belonging to somebody else no longer living.

Zero snapped at me impatiently to put the ring on my finger. I did so. After that, I was Mrs Zero.

He opened the door and called in Marijane. She crept in apologetically, crabwise, hanging her head as

if she had committed some offence and now wanted
to be punished for it. Zero told her brusquely she
had been demoted to Half from her previous rank as
Senior Wife. She would henceforth be Half a Wife,
a rank she would share with Betty Louella, so that
together they would make up a whole. This meant
they must divide Zero's attentions between them.
Whereas I was to become Number One, since I was
both the oldest in age and the newest by acquisition.
At that, Marijane wailed hugely and beat her head
against the wall. But Zero picked her up bodily and
carried her to the bunk room and deposited her there
on the floor, to be rid of her. Then he resumed his
rituals. He seized Emmeline, the wife of the night,
by the hair and drew her towards him. When I saw he
did not intend his most recent marriage to disrupt the
ordered sequence of his routine, I quickly slipped out
of his study while Emmeline removed her dungarees.
The next day, in a ceremonial containing an element
of gratified envy, they cut off all my long, yellow
hair and burned it in the stove so that now I had a
neat, Dutch doll hair-cut just as they did and I was
issued with a similar pair of dungarees.

   That was my initiation into the harem. Next day,
I took stock of my new surroundings.

   Historicity in America goes more quickly, jigs to
a more ragged rhythm than the elegiac measures
of the old world and so the ruins of this miners'
town, though it had been built no longer ago than
my own great grandmother's lifetime, looked, in
the analytic light of the desert, far older than the
rocks on which it had been built, with its desiccated

timbers and dishevelled roofs of iron, and far more poignant than a more ancient ruin because the wreck retained so much common humanity about it. The men who haphazardly put this town together had never intended it to transcend time, as the towns of Europe were built to do; they had left the town entirely at Time's untender mercy. It was still full of small panhandler's mementos, Tin-plate advertisements for corn-cure and hair-restorer hung by single nails from the clapboard sides of the old grocery. Bits and pieces of Americana decorated our dormitory in the ranch-house – a silent cuckoo clock, a framed photograph of a gold-rush mother. There was a pot-bellied, wood-burning stove in the kitchen and a rocking chair on the verandah in which Zero would often relax for a smoke, like an old-timer himself.

There were the ruins of a saloon with a long bar on which Zero howled and danced his poems that utilised all the revolutionary propaganda of the scream and sometimes he made his women dance, too. Behind the bar was a broken mirror with a sand-caked gilt frame and glass so freckled I could hardly make out New Eve's reflection in it for, in this mirror, she looked as if she were wearing an antique bridal veil. The roof was half gone and the softly whispering sand encroached everywhere on the splintered floorboards. In the ruins of an old chapel, under a sagging roof of corrugated iron, Zero kept his pigs.

Pigs were sacred to Zero. They were by no means confined to the filthy straw of their sty; Zero let

them run about the place just as they pleased,
so that often a gross sow would push open the
half-door of the kitchen with its snout and lumber,
squeaking hideously, over to the pot that bubbled
on the stove, knock it to the floor with one blow
of its clever cloven hoof and devour the steaming
contents as they swam in the gravy. We were not
allowed to shoo away the pigs nor the chorus of
piglets that snared our feet to trip us up everywhere
we went, or Zero would beat us. Nor would he
let us eat them; useless mouths, the twenty vicious
beasts dominated the life of the community, which
took its tone from their farouche manners.

When one of the sows littered, Marijane told
me, the girls had to steal away a piglet from the
udder, dress it up in baby-clothes (for trunks full of
babyclothes were kept in the women's dormitory,
ready for the unguessable but longed-for time when
the girls would mother a new breed of Americans),
dandle it on their knees, lullaby it and feed it with
warmed goats' milk from a rubber-nippled bottle.
In this way, the girls learned the disciplines of
motherhood.

He did not let us keep his pigs clean. He only
honoured them because they were gross. Coated
with their own muck, each pig stank like a cess-pit
and lolled about the place like a lord of creation,
with malice glinting in its little eyes. Zero allowed
his pigs a liberty he denied his wives and the pigs
took full advantage of it; they teased us unmercifully.
Often they would buffet us as we poured the buckets
full of food into their trough, so that we would

tumble headfirst into the steaming, bubbling mess
and emerge dripping, wiping the vegetable juice
from our eyes. They loved to trip us up when we
were carrying the clean laundry in from the drying
poles so we and our loads would fall, splat! into a
steaming puddle of pig-shit and we would have to
wash ourselves thoroughly under the icy water of
the pump and all the work be done again. Once,
Betty Louella told me, she discovered a sow in
farrow in the women's dormitory, in labour on her
own mattress, and Zero ordered her to play midwife
just as if the sow had been a human mother so all
was hot water and solicitude even though it was a
Saturday night and Betty Louella was deprived of
her weekly injection of Zero's tool because she had
to look after the lying-in.

But, if he let the pigs do as he pleased, he demanded
absolute subservience from his women. Although
"subservience" is the wrong word: they gave in to
him freely, as though they knew they must be wicked
and so deserve to be inflicted with such pain.

In the morning, when the first light of dawn
leaked in through the random curtains at the broken
windows, Betty Louella, or, if it were her turn in
Zero's bed, the next youngest, would roll from the
mattresses on which we slept hugger-mugger, all
together, and go out to the pump to draw water for
Zero's coffee, slyly shooing out of the kitchen any
pig who had crept in during the night – we could
not shoo loudly, in case Zero heard us and beat us.
The creaking of the ancient pump roused us all and up
we sprang to split the kindling; light the stove; go out

for eggs from the squawking chickens, comforting
our frozen hands in their blood-warm feathers as we
reached for the shelled fruit they'd dropped during
the night. Then some of us prepared flapjacks with
oatmeal scooped out of a spilling sack in the kitchen,
while others fed the holy pigs a lavish meal.

We made a heaping tray of breakfast for Zero
and, prompt at eight by the cuckoo-clock, the
door of his room opened and his bed-mate of the
previous night came out to fetch the tray and also
a bowl of chopped beefsteak for the lurcher. Cain
jumped into the bed when the girl came out of
it and took his first meal of the day in bed with
Master. But the wife, demoted to the ranks with
the morning, ate her breakfast in the kitchen with
the rest of us, a meal terminated the moment Zero
clanged his handbell to summon someone to fetch
his tray.

He took great pleasure in forcing us to eat our
breakfasts in an indigestible hurry and always rang
his bell so soon after we sat down that we hardly
had the time to gobble a single biscuit and, if we did
not eat then, we must go hungry until lunch-time,
since Zero forbade snacks between meals on pain
of the lash.

Now that Betty Louella and Marijane were both
Seven, to them fell the envied task of giving Zero his
morning blanket bath and in they'd trot, carrying
the vat of steaming water between them. But he'd never
take his trousers off in front of them; they'd soap
and lather his back and his chest and his armpits and
then they always had to turn their faces to the wall

and contemplate the effigy of Tristessa while he let his leather pants down and gave his private parts a quick flannelling himself. Though it wasn't his prick he wished to conceal, it was his amputated stump. When he was washed, combed and dressed all but for his boot, one by one we would file into him as he sat enthroned on his swivel chair in his study and each kiss his naked foot. He would bark, or grunt, or squeak, or mew at us because he only used the language of the animals towards his wives unless there was a very exceptional emergency and we had to answer in kind. If he did not like the tone of our response, he would savage the offender unmercifully with his bullwhip. So our first words every morning were spoken in a language we ourselves could not understand; but he could. Or so he claimed, and, because he ruled the roost and his word was law, it came to the same thing. So he regulated our understanding of him and also our understanding of ourselves in relation to him.

After we had kissed his solitary foot, we set about our tasks.

We watered the vegetable garden. His ranch-house was circled by a gap-toothed fence and, within this fence, lay the plot we girls watered daily, bearing dripping buckets from the pump. The watered ground was fertile enough to mock the aridity around it with its rich produce of fruit, cannabis and vegetables that soon ripened in the inevitable sun. We tended the domestic animals. The chickens lived in the hulk of a Model T Ford that lay where it had broken down in the dust long before any of us had

been born. There were goats of a devilish-looking
breed with black, silken hair and horns that curled
over their eyes. The goats were forbidden entry
into the garden. If a girl were careless enough to
let one slip through and gorge on the bean row
or the cabbage patch, she would be beaten and the
goat itself would be dispatched with one of Zero's
throwing knives. Then we would have a rare treat
of goat stew for a few days, though the incisorless
condition of the girls meant the meat must be cooked
to a pulp before they could eat it. After the pelt of
the goat was cured, we would have another blanket
to sleep on. Pelts in the process of curing hung in
the sun from a line in the drying ground where
we put out the laundry; they added their stench
to the ripe odour of the ordure of the pigs. The
goats provided milk, from which we occasionally
made ill-fated attempts to manufacture cheese, but
it never turned out right, always maggoty.

We cleaned the stolen cars he kept, like a sleek
herd of draught beasts, in a compound behind the
ranch-house, washed the clothes, prepared the food.
Once a week, on Wednesdays, two girls would take
out a car to make a garbage run to the supermarket
in a town some thirty jolting miles away, for our
plain fare of vegetables, grains, eggs, goats' milk
and the occasional meal of pulped chicken or goat
was eked out by the contents of bins of spoiled
food and leftovers we found on a concrete loading
platform at the rear entrance, waiting to be taken
to the refuse tip. There would be hands of green
bananas; blocks of veinous suet; softening bricks

of ice-cream; mice-nibbled wedges of cellophane-wrapped imported cheese, rare treats, gorgonzola, brie, gruyère; packs of butter only a little rancid – the huge plastic bins were cornucopias that spilled a rotten plenty, on which we feasted. After we'd cleared the refuse bins, we'd buy Zero and his dog their meat from the butchery counter. For, if we ate what the pigs did, our master and Cain the lurcher got good red meat three times a day and the girls paid honest money out for it from the cash they'd earned peddling their asses in Los Angeles. That summer, all seven of them spent three months on the game in the city, they told me, in order to save up enough money to keep Zero and his familiar well-fed throughout the winter.

And, by the time the winter was over, they believed the cities would all have broken open like boils. Then they would retire completely into the well-fortified ranch and live off their own produce until the riots were over. During this season of civil war, Zero would at last find out Tristessa's hiding place and her ravishment, then death, would restore the procreativity to his virility. My heart stopped for a moment when I heard that, though I knew quite well that all his rage of howling was directed towards Tristessa. His paranoia took this shadow for its focus. Certain hissing sibilants he would emit at the climaxes of his frenzies were almost on the point of becoming her serpentine name, as if he were spitting her out in his unfruitful orgasms.

After this fecund murder, Zero would descend on Los Angeles in his helicopter and they would be able to take exactly what they pleased from the freezer cabinets without paying one dime for it and they would live in a penthouse in the abandoned city and watch colour television all day and start to repopulate the suddenly barren continent, now empty of all but the tribe of Zero.

They believed all this would happen because Zero had told them that was the way it would be. He'd sung and danced his variation of Götterdämmerung on the bar in the old saloon for them so often they were sure it must be true. Each one of the wives – Marijane; Sadie; Apple Pie; Tiny; Betty Boop; Betty Louella; Emmeline – repeated this story to me, always with the same radiant conviction, and I was forced, in the end, to believe they believed it as though it were revealed scripture. Then an awful pity for them overcame me; these poor girls had indeed dedicated themselves, body, heart and soul, to the Church of Zero.

As I washed dishes with Emmeline or hoed rows of turnips with Betty Louella, I tried to explain something of the real state of the world, though I could speak only in a very low voice for fear Zero might hear me, or one of the girls betray me to him in sign language – there was very little feeling of camaraderie among them, they were always betraying one another to a beating. But whoever I was talking to would soon smile at me the tolerant, patronising smile one uses to foolish children, tell me I would understand everything in Zero's good time and, besides, I shouldn't be talking, anyway, since it was against Zero's law.

Their common passion for the one-eyed, one-legged monomaniac predicated their conviction in his myth and since belief was the proof of love, each girl strived to outdo all the others in the strength of her conviction because they fretfully competed amongst themselves all the time for more than their fair share of his attentions. But his myth depended on their conviction; a god-head, however shabby, needs believers to maintain his credibility. Their obedience ruled him. All the girls had the same dreary biographies; broken homes, remand homes, parole officers, maternal deprivation, inadequate father figures, drugs, pimps, bad news. They were case histories, rather than women. They loved Zero for his air of authority but only their submission had created that. By himself, he would have been nothing. Only his hatred of them kept them enthralled. And they pretended to believe, for his sake, that a weakly injection of his holy if sterile fluid kept them from all the ills of the flesh and they would have been unable to survive without it.

We lived as women of the Mormons must have done, in the appearance of a state of terminal bondage, inhabitants of the ranch-house and the ruined township that surrounded it, a gross parody of pioneers; and, for most of the time, we were stoned, smashed, sweet-cured in grass smoke. How else could we have survived it? The boredom, the pigs, the toil, the bad food, the fleas, the hard beds, constant beatings, deprived of speech . . . Yet grass and Zero's rhetoric transformed this world. The ranch-house was Solomon's Temple; the ghost town was the New Jerusalem; the helicopter his chariot of fire, his prick his bow of burning gold, etc etc etc.

On my trips into town, I foraged for old newspapers and peeked at them in secret; if Zero'd known I was looking for information about the outside world, he'd have flayed me alive. From the damp, stained sheets I found tucked among the garbage, I learned that the Siege of Harlem continued but the Western press relegated it to the lower headlines of the inner pages and paid far more attention to the exploits of the National Guard in the law and order riots in the cities of the Pacific Coast. California was opting for secession from the Union; was the nation on the brink of Civil War? The President, in a frenzy, issued contradictory statements on relations with China. Yet the supermarket continued to do business although, at each visit, we found the garbage grew less sumptuous.

I was sustained by this however fleeting contact with a world outside the deathly and annihilating circle of Zero; when I was at home among the girls, I kept as silent as I could and tried to imitate the way they moved and the way they spoke for I knew that, in spite of Sophia's training in Beulah, I would often make a gesture with my hands that was out of Eve's character or exclaim with a subtly male inflection that made them raise their eyebrows. This intensive study of feminine manners, as well as my everyday work about the homestead, kept me in a state of permanent exhaustion. I was tense and preoccupied; although I was a woman, I was now also passing for a woman, but, then, many women born spend their whole lives in just such imitations.

However, the result of my apprenticeship as a woman was, of course, that my manner became a little too emphatically feminine. I roused Zero's suspicions because I began to behave *too much* like a woman and he started to watch me warily for signs of the tribade. If he had spied any, or surprised me fingering any of his girls, he would have shot me. His hatred of female homosexuality was inflexible; it was obsessional. And poor, beautiful, intangible Tristessa, was she not the Queen of Dykes; had she not dried up the desert, made it all sand, he said one night when he was drunk. I think Zero must have picked up some distorted rumour about Beulah, unless there was some other women's commune in the desert he might have heard of, and speculated about; he fed his paranoia on rumours until his head was full of strange notions that cross-fertilised one another and ingeniously produced reams of fresh, false, self-contradictory but passionately believed information. He no longer needed news of the world, since he manufactured it himself to his own designs.

But, in spite of, or, perhaps, because of his suspicion I might be too much of a woman for him, he took a great fancy to me and our marital encounters, therefore, took place at a pitch of intensity that filled me with terror. Each time, a renewed defloration, as if his violence perpetually refreshed my virginity. And more than my body, some other yet equally essential part of my being was ravaged by him for, when he mounted me with his single eye blazing like the mouth of an automatic, his little body imperfectly stripped, I felt myself to be, not myself but he; and the experience of this crucial lack of self, which always brought with it a shock of introspection, forced me to know myself as a former violator at the moment of my own violation. When he entered me, the act seemed to me one of seppuku, a ritual disembowelment I committed upon myself, although I was only watching him and only felt my pain and unpleasure in his joy at my pain and pleasure at my distress.

So I lived in the dormitory at the ranch-house, tended the pigs and made the garbage run; while every Sunday night, I suffered the rage of his marital rape. My life as the wife of Zero! Boredom, pain, a state of siege.

"I am Zero," he said in a rare burst of speech, after he'd been eyeing the bust of Nietzsche one night for some hours. "The lowest point; vanishing point; nullity. I am the freezing point in Centigrade and my wives experience the flame of my frigidity as passion."

But I'd have said he was the king of a rainy country, powerful yet impotent, since his power depended on his dependants. And impotent he certainly was. Marijane had a child in a foster-home in New Hampshire but by Zero she had no child, although she had lived with him for two whole years. Sadie had had four abortions but not the chance of one since she married Zero. The ranch-house was as much the realm of sterility as the desert that surrounded it. Here, only the pigs brought forth. How poignant it was, that Zero should make his wives dress the piglets up in white lace bonnets and dandle them on their knees! Yet it was a great relief to me to know I would not be betrayed to motherhood in this vile place.

Zero's routine was rigid, though not unvarying. For example, he'd always spent the entire day combing the desert for signs of Tristessa until some black-clad desert dwellers, probably from a rival community, had shot at the whirly bird one morning; now he waited until night protected him, for he was a well-disguised but habitual coward. When I heard about this incident, I remembered how Sophia had fired at a helicopter and knew Zero must have shot that mysterious, enormous bird, out of pure envy because it had been so beautiful.

In the mornings, after we'd kissed his foot, before we brought him his dinner, he sat on his rocking chair on the verandah smoking grass and scribbling on the pale air the outlines of epics of dissociated noise. He occupied the afternoons with his draw; but when, towards five o'clock, he grew bored with shooting down his tin cans – for he never missed one, so the exercise held no element of surprise for him – he would order the girls to stop whatever we were doing, go to the bunkhouse and rummage in the trunks of costumes he kept there for us. It was time for the poetry recital.

Those trunks contained shoes with pointed heels five or six inches high; boots that laced to the crotch;

stockings of sheer silk or coarse mesh; tinselled cache-sexes of every kind; and tassles, which we attached to our bare nipples. There were also wigs, to conceal our pudding-basin haircuts. Each of us would select whatever garments appealed to us from this trove, he allowed us that much autonomy, and then we would all stream to the bar to dress ourselves, twittering with excitement at this opportunity to please him. When we were dressed up, or undressed, in the style of high pornography, he would make us line up on the bar and dance to the music of his transistorised cassette set.

Since the only tapes he possessed were of the music of Wagner, we performed our high kicks in ragged unison to Siegfried's journey down the Rhine or the love duet from Tristan or the ride of the Valkyrie. He played the music very loudly, until the burnished coverlid of the sky seemed to clang in sonorous sympathy, like a gong struck with a padded stick. I was the worst dancer in the world, as you can imagine, and I dreaded these occasions for I would remember watching Leilah watch herself in the mirror and now I sensed all the lure of that narcissistic loss of being, when the face leaks into the looking-glass like water into sand.

Then Zero would take the centre of the stage, while we supplied him with a sort of visible refrain, and he would dance out the violation and death of Tristessa, followed by the subsequent apotheosis of Zero. This was the unique matter of his drama. He leaped and danced and ululated like a dervish or a Tom o' Bedlam on top of the dusty bar in the saloon that now only the pigs, as if they were the ghosts of thirsty miners, frequented; at the climax of these exhibitions of poetry, he would faint, for he expended enormous amounts of energy upon them. What a performance! He roared, ranted, ramped, sweated and shrieked while we girls cheered; then, suddenly, he'd drop like a felled tree, so we would have to carry him to his bed and feed him bourbon from a liquor-soaked cloth nipple we pressed in his mouth. When he was rested and recovered, it would be time for supper. He'd eat in his room and, afterwards, by the benign, mothering light of the hanging oil lamp, with his dog's head on his knee and a bottle of bourbon ready for sipping on his desk, a joint smouldering in the onyx ashtray, he scrutinised maps of the desert, pored over them endlessly, to find out where his nest of dykes might be, so that he could descend on them in his winged chariot of wrath and eliminate them all, blast from the earth the infamous Tristessa, Witch, bitch and Typhoid Mary of sterility.

She'd blasted his seed because he was Masculinity incarnate, you see. Utilising various cabbalistic devices, Tristessa had magicked away his reproductive capacity via the medium of the cinema screen. On our mattresses in the secret nights, the girls whispered to me how he'd been watching her in a revival of *Emma Bovary* in an art-house in Berkeley and Tristessa's eyes, eyes of a stag about to be gralloched, had fixed directly upon his and held them. He'd been on mescaline; she'd grown, grown to giant size, and her eyes consumed him in a ghastly epiphany. He'd felt a sudden, sharp, searing pain in his balls. With visionary certainty, he'd known the cause of his sterility. He was like a man who could not cast a shadow, and that was because Tristessa had sucked his shadow clean away. Wow, said Marijane, would you ever believe. . . Yet she believed it; or said she did.

Before Zero'd lost his eye – poked out by a broomstick in a brawl with a warder during one of his spells in prison – he'd been a great reader of fan mags. He'd thoroughly researched Tristessa. On the cluttered shelves of his study were pile upon pile of yellowing magazines the pages of which the desert air made crisp and friable, like enormous potato chips. These magazines dated back before we were all born, had been obtained from dealers in ephemerae all over the West Coast. All contained pictures of Tristessa. Her favourite food was black raspberry ice-cream; her favourite drink, Russian tea. Her favourite colour, her favourite composer, beige and Tchaikovsky. Already she liked best, on vacation, to go into the desert. She had a hideaway retreat in Arizona staffed, it was rumoured, by a butler who was a deaf-mute; the location of this hideaway was Hollywood's best kept secret except for one, a secret even better kept which we would discover for ourselves after we'd solved the first secret.

But all these scraps and snippets were surmises or inventions of ingenious public relations officers, for she never gave interviews, she was notorious for that. She was famous for her silences. A scurrilous paper-back ghosted autobiography printed some

time in the fifties hinted grossly she was a tribade
but it had been published long after her retirement,
of course. Perhaps this pseudo-fact had sewn the
seed of Zero's monumental obsession. Yet it was
true that not a single one of the million upon million
words heaped upon her and her memory gave even
the remotest hint she had known any man at all,
except in the most abstract and social sense.

And nobody knew where she was, you see.
Nobody at all. The books and magazines all agreed
on that. She was alive and well but she'd become perfectly invisible. When she was forty, she abandoned
Hollywood and went into a retirement so conventual
no newshound in all the world could flush her out
of it. All she let be known was, she was living in
a desert place, and had taken up sculpture in glass,
and the deaf-mute remained her only companion.

On moonlight nights, away we went, in search
of Tristessa. Even the weakest moon sent Zero out
on his quest. We'd all pile into the 'copter, be up and
away on just such a reconnoitring expedition as the
one on which they'd happened upon me. And after
moonfall, of course, the wife of the night had her
batteries recharged with Zero's magic fluid. That was
another invariable. All the whispered conversations I
had with my co-wives took place on our mattresses
in the dark dormitory while the sounds of Zero's
copulations rang through the thin wall. We could
hear every thrust, grunt and moan and the noises
excited some of the poor girls with such erotic envy
their hands would creep helplessly to their slits and
sometimes to one another's. I was astonished to

discover that, if Zero found out, he would have lined them up against the saloon wall and shot them. But, all the same, they went out dyke-hunting with him on moony nights as if nothing at all had happened. But there it was. These practices were an inevitable concomitant of harem life and the wives excused them to themselves by, when the sun came up and they were themselves again, pretending nothing whatsoever had happened.

As Zero's passion for me ran its course, it did not grow less but it grew bewildered. Something in me rang false; he knew it by some atavistic intuition. One Sunday night, after he brusquely ordered me to undress, he took it into his head to examine me with almost a jeweller's eye; he could have been inspecting a diamond he feared might be flawed. He made me stand on the desk and poked the barrel of a rifle in my ribs to make me turn round and round. Then he made me lie down on his bed, where he went over me point by point, breasts, belly, the junction of the thighs, knees, feet, the gaps between the toes, everywhere. He made me crouch on my knees and elbows and peered up my asshole; he told me I had too much hair around it and he also took exception to my hips, although their width was no fault of mine, Mother had widened the pelvis by means of bone grafts to facilitate the exit of the new Messiah.

With the ears of my imagination, I heard the girls stirring with vicarious lust beyond the wooden wall and I was very much afraid in case he found a flaw in my disguise, that Mother might have left some unknown-to-me clue impressed in my new flesh that showed I'd been reupholstered and, a few short months before, just as much of a man as Zero. More of a man, in fact; hadn't my manhood sent Leilah off to the Haitian abortionist? Yet, when he righted me again, I saw, in spite of his little jibes, almost pure envy in his eyes for Mother had made me unnatural only in that I was perfect. Venus herself had risen from the surgery.

It was this perfection of physical beauty that puzzled Zero, even scared him, so that now, to master his fear, he attacked me until I thought I would die of it, so furious were his exertions, while the girls in hell outside his bed groaned so loudly I was sure he could hear them, too, and I began to cry, to drown the noise they were making and spare them a beating.

No. I'm lying. I cried because of the pain he caused me; my renewed eyes seemed to have been made of water, since often they would leak.

A range of mountains had curtailed his search throughout that winter. Jutting through the shifting flesh of the desert, they were capped with snow, hooded with mist throughout the cold months, dangerous, impassable. But, as the weather grew warmer, Zero clenched with decision; he would fly over the mountains as soon as the snows melted, for he had combed the entire desert with no success and was now quite sure Tristessa must live beyond those frozen peaks.

I had spent three months as a wife of Zero. It was as savage an apprenticeship in womanhood as could have been devised for me and, if Mother had selected me, however arbitrarily, to atone for the sins of my first sex vis-à-vis my second sex via my sex itself, I would say that, by the time the chaste and delirious spring awakened all manner of plants that love dry places from the sand and began to warm the nights a little, I had become almost the thing I was. The mediation of Zero turned me into a woman. More. His peremptory prick turned me into a savage woman.

When he laid me down on his bed, I could have torn out his eyes if he had not started to bind my wrists together when I began to show too much turbulence. His wives, with their faces of ancient children, who so innocently consented to be less than human, filled me with an angry pity. When I saw their skins were often greenish due to the beatings he inflicted on them, I was moved by an anger they were too much in love with him to feel. My anger kept me alive.

The news in the dank papers I scavenged at the supermarket grew more and more grim as the winter receded. They'd used bombs, in the end, to break the Siege of Harlem and the blacks had retaliated with a series of political assassinations. The State of California was implementing its decision to secede. The pickings in the garbage were scantier than ever; no treats of suppurating camembert, now. Zero's supply of gasoline was running low but he was too delirious to show any anxiety, though he may have felt time was running out for now he abandoned his habitual routine to fly every day, all day long with the dog his only companion, scouring the mountains and beyond them and he often left his wives behind, he was a lone scout, now.

Every day, he creaked a little further over the mountains in his dilapidated old whirlybird; she lay on the other side, did she not? His holy grail, his quest, in the desert she'd spawned, across the ribs of rock. Sometimes he'd go out one morning and not return until the next; we'd be completely forgotten in the heat of the hunt! The girls acknowledged that Zero's sacred quest must take precedence over their needs, he'd service us as soon as he had a moment . . . but, such was his zeal, those moments became rarer and rarer. The routine of the ranch was quite disrupted. The imminence of the apocalypse set us all on edge. We'd wait breathlessly for his return. And when he returned, his clothes filled with dust, the echoes of a wild surmise in his eyes, he'd thrust us away from him with his bullwhip as we came clustering round for his news, to crash on to his mattress in his study in the dreamless sleep of exhaustion. And not one ounce of elixium vitae for any of us. But we comforted ourselves with the thought that soon, soon! it would be elixium vitae indeed.

One day, when Apple Pie and Tiny went to collect the garbage, they found the plastic containers all empty. The store was closed and discontented tradespeople stood in fretful clumps in the street for the town, it seemed, had eaten its cupboard bare and there was no food left. The girls had been frightened by the ominous crowds and the low rattle of gun-fire in the backstreets. They came directly home and, as

they were telling us their adventures in the kitchen
and we were congratulating ourselves on the garden
and the goats and the sacks of grain, the sputtering
roar of the helicopter announced Zero's return. He
came straight to the kitchen. He was so exalted
with triumph he consented to speak to us in plain
English.

"It glittered," he said. "I saw it. The Witches'
lair."

He pulled his pistol from its holster and emptied
the barrels through the roof, so that we were all
showered with dust and splinters, the startled pigs
squealed like a slaughterhouse and the late afternoon
sun flooded in and made us blink.

Nine

The cold winds of solitude blew about her house: solitude and melancholy, said Tristessa, that is a woman's life. I went towards you as towards my own face in a magnetic mirror, but when, in accordance with all the laws of physics, you came towards me, I did not feel a sense of homecoming, only the forlorn premonition of loss.

I exhibited all the symptoms of panic when I met you – pallor, shallow breathing, a prickle of cold sweat. It was like finding myself on the brink of an abyss but the giddiness that seized me and shook me and would not let me go sprang from a cause I did not understand, then – that the abyss on which you opened was that of my self, Tristessa.

You were an illusion in a void. You were the living image of the entire Platonic shadow show, an illusion that could fill my own emptiness with marvellous, imaginary things as long as, just so long as, the movie lasted, and then all would all vanish. This world had never been sufficient for you; to go beyond the boundaries of flesh had been your occupation and so you had become nothing, a wraith that left only traces of a silver powder on the hands that clutched helplessly at your perpetual vanishings.

The whirring helicopter hovered over a crag where eagles nested. Below us, the wan fingers of the dying moon polished the heaped glass hoops of her home and made them shine as if the house possessed its own, cold light, like the emissions of those fish who live at the bottom of the sea and talk to one another in a language of submarine luminescence we find so mysterious only because it is perfectly transparent. The harem squeaked and gibbered at the spectacle as down we plummeted, to land inside the high wall with which she surrounded herself, in a park full of trees beside a dark, thickly scummed swimming pool as long and as wide as a little lake. It must have been fed by some subterranean spring, for its waters had the sullen look of unimaginable depth; very high above it quivered the taut strut of a diving board.

So the helicopter touched down on a fractured terrace where weeds reared up through the cracks in the concrete. But this terrace, although it was deserted, was not uninhabited. Grand transparencies lodged there – swollen, tear-shaped forms of solid glass with dimples and navels and blind depressions in their sides, the abortions of expressive surfaces. Some were as tall as I and weeds and creepers had anchored them to the ground; others had tumbled on their sides and shattered when they hit the concrete. But, though they were of all kinds of sizes and each one subtly different from the other, all were, more or less, the shape of tears and had been scattered plentifully, as in a passion of grief, all around the margins of the deep, black reach of desert-locked water.

As soon as we tumbled out of our craft, Zero tossed a stone at one of these mute presences; it burst immediately, in a shower of shards, and the harem busily set to to smash all the others.

Evidence of a curious technology was assembled along the poolside. There was a portable furnace, in which the fire had been put out for the night; buckets and containers in neat piles; and an enormous skip full of sand, freshly imported from the desert. The diving board dripped icicles of glass and a solid frosting of glass clung to the rungs of the ladder that led up to it. All was neat, everything was tidy. There was a broom propped next to the skip and the concrete had been swept clean before work for the day had stopped. But everything was in perfect order for work to begin again the next day and the day after that and the day after, days like glass beads on a string of duration. Her work was endless, she carried tubs and cauldrons and pails of heat-blasted sand, sand blasted into liquid glass, up the ladder that had vitrified where her bucket splashed, and tipped the liquid glass into the swimming pool, where, at the touch of water, it turned into her huge, solid tears.

But now her eyeless glass menhirs were all broken; how satisfied the farouche young girls were! The ghost of her moonlit house trembled in the water, tier upon round tapering tier of glass and steel diminishing upwards to a point we could not see. She lived in her own wedding cake, had burrowed deeply into its interior.

She lived in her own mausoleum.

The reflection of her mausoleum vanished as the moon slid behind the cliff. All, now, was a perfect darkness and Zero lit us a clue with his flashlight and drew us tomb-robbers to a verandah where we tripped over scattered deck-chairs that must have been abandoned after a pool-side soirée when we were all babies. The canvas flapped from the rusted frames of café umbrellas tossed about on their sides on the ground. My foot turned on a rolling bottle. All abandoned, as if in the middle of a party, years ago, by a host suddenly sick of vanities, who had turned out all his guests like the cleansing of the Temple.

Only a few, gross, palpable invisibles of glass lived here now, like mineralised fruit, and Zero and the girls conscientiously broke them all.

The house rose above us in its ascending sequences of circular elevations, immense, echoing – cupping the darkness within its walls; before us were curved, sliding doors that led directly into a foyer and Zero beat upon them to announce our arrival. As soon as he touched the toughened glass, a burglar alarm went off with a rude roar that sent a crowd of birds who had been roosting on the glass arcades into the air, squawking with pique. After a while, within the house, we saw the reticent flicker of a candle-flame that halted, wavering, some distance from the door. There was a whirr, a click and a

crackle; an electronic voice stated categorically; NO
ADMITTANCE, NOT EVEN ON BUSINESS.

Zero swung his shotgun and blasted the thick glass
panels. They shattered. The remote candle-flame
danced and vanished; a blast of dank, cold perfume
issued from the jagged holes he had made. He fired
another round: the girls picked their way into the
building through these abrupt apertures and now
we all produced our little flash-lights and sent the
beams spinning round the glass entrance hall.

The surfaces flashed reciprocally in the intermittent
light, for the couches and low tables, here, were
all made of glass and chromium plate. Spiders had
woven their vague trapezes between the friable heads
of dead peonies in enormous glass jars streaked with
tide marks where the water had evaporated long ago.
Soft clouds of dust rose from the yellowed pelts of
polar bears flung on the floor and their mummified
heads roared mutely at us in balked fury. The walls
of this long, low, serpentine room were made of
glass tiles, so we could see the undersides of more
furniture upstairs, and here and there the back of
another rug – all dim and subtly distorted. Yet
the dark spaces, full of the desolate scent of
time and old perfume, had the air of a long-
abandoned cathedral, for it was just as cold, just
as quiet, and the furniture, on its own, under
the influence of the tensions of its structure, now
and then let out a faint, melodious twang as
if it had been touched by a ghostly fingernail.

When I heard the faint music the house made
by itself, I felt myself already in the presence of

Tristessa, as if she were one of those super-sensitive ghosts who manifest their presence by only a sound, an odour, or an impression of themselves that they leave on the air behind them – a sense, a feeling that, for no definable reason, penetrates us with a pure anguish, as if they were telling us, in the only way left to them, that is, by a direct intervention upon our sensibilities, how much, how very much they want to be alive and how impossible it is for them to be so.

Through the shifting perspectives of glass, among the reflections that danced in my thin beam of light, I saw the spiral staircase that was the core of the house rearing up towards the sky like the central stem of a plant.

Nobody had entered this room for years, for decades. Dust drifted dreamily upwards from the magazines when Marijane touched them – fan-mags and movie mags with pictures of women with bland, oval faces and plucked eyebrows. The swinging arc of Zero's torch waked nothing but the sonorities of silence in this echoing place, that gave us no hint of the source of the candle-flame that had flickered a response to our arrival.

At first, Zero and the girls were all very quiet, as if this hushed, neglected glamour startled and even awed them, but soon they began to behave in a more extroverted manner. Marijane dropped her dungarees, squatted and deposited a spreading pool of urine on the floor that was made of glass tiles, and after that they all felt more at home although the cold struck me to the bone so that my teeth chattered and I could not join in their frolics as they played tag among the furniture and tumbled the desiccated blossoms from the flower-arrangements.

Then, with a jolt that flung all of us on to our faces on the floor, the whole house shuddered and creaked; and, as it creaked, it began to revolve – yes, revolve! – slowly on a mysterious axle deep in the earth beneath us. The girls squeaked and shrieked as at a miracle or a landslide and hid their heads in the bearskin rugs. Zero recovered his self-possession and his balance first; he staggered erect and brandished his gun at whatever invisible mechanism it might be that now, with increasing momentum, began to spin us around as if we were all on a merry-go-round. He and his dog began a frenzied search of the ground floor and I alone ran after him, because I had some notion of protecting the chatelaine of the house from him when he found her.

Zero spotted an open metal door banging above a metal staircase that went downwards. It might have led to the engine room of a ship and down we plunged, all three, with the barking dog in the van. The staircase span round with the house but we ourselves jumped off it on to terra firma, for now we were underground, in the unmoving underpinning of the house.

We found ourselves in an extensive basement. We roared through a laundry room where dirty linen was piled on the floor in pale, slithering mounds; through a small, domestic gymnasium with wall-bars and a vaulting horse; discovered a monstrous garbage disposal unit; a dark-walled projection room with

disordered chairs and a floor covered with empty
bottles, glasses, syringes.

Then we came to a door locked on the inside.
Zero shot through the lock and we discovered a
tiny, withered Oriental in a swing chair at a control
panel, crouching over a wheel that looked like the
driving wheel of a car. He wore flannel pyjamas
and a black silk kimono flung over them; when he
opened his mouth to shout, no sound came out and
he swung round in his chair to defend himself with
a dainty, pearl-handled revolver but, before he could
fire, Zero spattered him all across the driving cabin
and grasped hold of the wheel himself. But however
hard he twisted it, nothing stopped or made the house
spin faster, so I guessed the Oriental had somehow
locked the wheel before he died; now we revolved
at a dizzy speed and ominous creaks indicated the
mechanism had not been used for years and might
shudder the whole glass-house to smithereens if we
continued our frolics within it.

Though Zero pushed every button, pressed every
switch on the control panel, nothing changed the
motion of the house, no lights came on – nothing
at all happened, except that the house suddenly filled
with very loud music when he pushed a button
shaped like a crotchet.

It was the music from *Gone With The Wind*, the
Tara theme . . . I recognised it immediately, but
because this ingenious mechanism had been installed
long before the introduction of long-playing records
or tape recordings, the music lasted for only three
and a half minutes at a time and there was a rasping

click between each sequence of soaring strings. Zero turned the volume of the music as high as it would go, then we clambered back up the staircase.

He ordered the girls to fan out and search for Tristessa herself, who must be skulking somewhere in this spinning, transparent labyrinth that was now full of the protracted hiccups of cheap music – a juddering silence imposed itself upon us every three and a half minutes as, somewhere in the viscera of the house, a bakelite disc fell from a diminishing stack on to the growing pile beneath it, like a musical hour-glass. I will always remember Tristessa's theme from *Nastasya Fillipovna*, the slow movement of the Pathetic Symphony, how the strings caressed the house with aching, impotent hands – and how the mechanism jammed there. During the course of the night, the needle went round and round and round upon that one disc until the tooth of steel ground down at last and the bakelite was dug into deep grooves and the record sputtered more and more ineffectually until at last, by the time they crucified Tristessa, the music had diminished to no more than an asthmatic rumble.

But where was she – where was she hiding? How could she hide here, where everything was visible?

I tagged along behind Zero as he ran up the circular glass staircase into the darkness and we found ourselves in a strange place, the first of the circular galleries of which the house was composed. Night curtained the invisible walls. I saw the stars burning and the horizon wheeling. The strings shivered through hidden loudspeakers and here the air was thick with the smell of spice and incense. The beam of Zero's torch wandered through the darkness until it fastened upon, of all things, a bier of glass bearing a glass coffin and, inside the box, a corpse.

"Sheee-it!" exclaimed surprised Zero.

The occupant of the coffin was a young boy in a black leather jacket, zipped up to his chin; he wore blue jeans. On his feet were sneakers. A pair of dark glasses was propped on his nose. His hands were crossed upon a bouquet of white roses at his breasts and four unlit white candles stood in glass candlesticks around him. Zero dug in his pants' pocket to find a box of matches; he threw them to me and I lit the candles one by one. A greenish, mysterious light that cast enormous shadows filled the room. Zero seemed curiously discomposed in the presence of such a still and odorous death; he lifted the hinged lid of the glass box with an unexpected care, almost a tenderness. Slowly, cautiously he stretched out his hand to touch the pale forehead. His hand trembled.

He drew back with a start and an exclamation.

The corpse was not a corpse at all. It was a cunningly executed waxwork.

We looked about us and found we were in an entire hall of waxworks, all in coffins, all with candles at their heads and feet. These waxworks were executed with great fidelity in the detail. The translucent fingernails had been inserted with meticulous precision; each hair stuck individually into the scalp; the curve of each nostril was as sweet and perfect as that of a petal. At an unspoken command of Zero's, I went around the coffins lighting every candle.

Jean Harlow, in a clinging gown of white satin, lay beside James Dean, both of whom had died of fame; then I found Marilyn Monroe, stark naked, just as they found her on her death bed; and Sharon Tate, in a tide of golden hair, she, poor girl, stabbed to death by mad people; Ramon Navarro, beaten to death by intruders in his own home; Lupe Velez, died by her own hand; Valentino, consumption and loneliness; Maria Montez, boiled to death in her bath for vanity's sake; all the unfortunate dead of Hollywood lay here, with candles at their heads and feet and flowers on their still bosoms. The flowers, too, were made of wax.

Now the room was a blaze of candlelight and the figures looked more life-like than ever, as if we had stumbled into a cave where all these fabulous beings had retired, when their time on the screen was up, to sleep until the last trump wakened them. It was the Seven Sleepers' den but more than seven slept here. I, and even Zero, was struck by a kind of profane awe at the silence, the incense, the ensorcellated light, the simulated corpses boxed up in glass like very precious cakes.

Then I came to a bier set a little higher than the others, raised up on a glass platform.

This bier was an immense lump of cast glass frozen in the midst of its flowings that contained innumerable pellucid references to the spectrum within it. A branched candelabra at the head of the bed in the shape of a dropsical hand lit the woman who lay upon it with five tongues of fire after I put my match to the tapers at its fingertips. This woman lay on her bier without any cover over her; she was – I should have guessed it! – the lady of the house.

At first, I thought it must be her corpse, she alone dead among the effigies, a masterpiece of the embalmer's art – look! fine, dry lines on her forehead and a tiny wart on the index finger of the hand that clasped the white-satin-bound Bible on her breast. And she had chosen, in death, to lie surrounded by effigies, like a King of Ancient Egypt. Her face had in no way changed from the face I remembered, that magical oval, shaved eyebrows, cupid's bow painted over her own lips with her long hair tumbled about her as if she had not been laid out on the bed but had herself lain down and died there, in a chiffon négligé, clutching the Good Book. But her hair had turned white, like Rip Van Winkle's. Her prone frame was a little longer than I remembered but otherwise so like her own reflection on the screen it took my breath away; that spectacular wraith might have been only the invention of all our imaginations and yet, all the time, she had been real.

I experienced an extraordinary fugue of feeling when I saw her lying there upon her own bier. It was as if, like a drowning man, I relived my entire life up to that point in a single instant, so that I was again the child whose dreams she had invaded and also the young man for whom she had become the essence of nostalgia and yet I remained the thing I was, a young woman, New Eve, whose sensibility had been impregnated with that of Tristessa during the insomniac nights of transmutation in the desert. New Eve looked down, in an ecstasy of regret, at this sign of love made flesh she could not, now, possess, even if death had not possessed Tristessa first.

More than that. It was as if all Tristessa's movies were being projected all at once on that pale, reclining figure so I saw her walking, speaking, dying, over and over again in all the attitudes that remained in this world, frozen in the amber of innumerable spools of celluloid from which her being could be extracted and endlessly recycled in a technological eternity, a perpetual resurrection of the spirit.

I learned later that she called her waxwork collection the HALL OF THE IMMORTALS, and she herself would live as long as persistence of vision, would she not. She had cheated the clock in her castle of purity, her ice palace, her glass shrine. She was a sleeping beauty who could never die since she had never lived.

Even in death, she was enigmatic and let her corpse lie among ingenious simulacra of corpses.

I was very sad to see Tristessa dead, as I thought, and leaned over her, with the trepidation of a violator of graves, to tuck back a stray lock of her white hair, drifted like snow across her steep brow. Her eyelids were still and moist. I felt a warmth rise from her skin. I saw the delicate hairs in her nostrils quiver with the most fragile respiration. I let out my breath in a great gust of wonder. She now desperately continued her grand defiance;

she would cheat death, now, by pretending death.
What to do? How to help her?

But Zero's dog lolloped eagerly across the gallery,
propped his forepaws up on the side of her bed, nosed
the folds of her négligé inquisitively, then flung back
his head and howled. Zero, who had been occupying
himself opening the coffins, hurling the waxworks
to the ground and trampling upon them, turned.
Tristessa's eyelids flickered. The dog seized a fold
of her robe between his teeth and tugged. Just as
Zero hoisted up his sub-machine gun, Tristessa leapt
from the bed with extraordinary agility, seized the
lighted candelabra and flung her Bible at him with
such force it struck him full in the face and sent him
reeling. He staggered back and the staccato chatter
of his bullets drilled the ceiling as full of holes as
the nozzle of a watering-can. While his attention
was distracted, she darted from the room.

The dog, baying, immediately gave chase and
when the harem tumbled into the gallery, summoned
by the shooting, Zero was already in hot pursuit of
his prey and so was I, darting at his heels up the
spiral staircase, following those five winking nodes
of light round and round and round as the house
span on its endless, stationary journey, sobbing and
groaning to itself, and the reiterated strings ached
and mourned for the pity of it all at an immense
volume from many hidden speakers. The staircase
drove its upward corkscrew through endless galleries
that flashed briefly in the lights we carried. Round
and round we darted, until I was giddy. The glass
steps rang under Zero's boot heels and everything

around us was in motion. We seemed to be running against gravity to a peak of the world.

The staircase soared right up out of the house and ended in a round eyrie, like a crows' nest. The cold fresh air broke upon us like a wave.

She flung the candelabra over the metal railing; the candle flames blew out at once and there was a crashing tinkle as glass fell on glass far below. Her wings of lace blew about in the wind that raced around the spinning tower. She was poised on the parapet, about to plunge, as the beam of light from Zero's torch impaled her.

It was as if she could not stand light, as if she had been kept from light so long she could have crumbled at the touch of it, just as the embalmed bodies of the Ancient Egyptians disintegrate into dust when air touches them. She fell back on to the floor of the glass crows' nest and crouched against the parapet whimpering fearfully, covering her eyes with her too-white, over-undulent arms to keep the light out. The chiffon of her robe drifted down to the floor more slowly than she did. It hung on the air behind her for a little while, like a dying fall, then settled softly and comprehensively upon her, like snow, so that she was quite concealed but for her rustling mass of white hair that the wind moved.

Zero paid no attention to the poignancy of the spectacle and was by her side in two strides, although here, high up in the whizzing air, the house shuddered and rocked dreadfully and blew up a fierce wind by its passage. He seized her shoulder and wrenched her out of the tumbled plumage in which she was hiding. She moaned and tried to conceal her face behind the jewelled bars of fingers as long and thin and pale as sticks of canned asparagus but Zero tore her hands away and shone the flashlight full into her great, dazed, vacant eyes that seemed to be all black, depthless pupil. Her enormous eyes shifted about at random in their deep sockets. They moved like the eyes of the blind move, at the impulse of thought and not at that of vision so, try as I would, I could not imagine how she saw the world, what connections she made between looking and seeing.

She screamed. Her contorted face was wonderfully beautiful in its terror. She began to babble incoherently and enormous tears ran down her colourless cheeks. When he saw she was crying, Zero began to laugh at her so that I could have killed him because he had so carelessly tipped over Tristessa, that magic vase of sorrow, and let its freight of woe come spilling out.

Tall, pale, attenuated enigma, your face an invitation to necrophilia, face of an angel upon a tombstone, a face that will haunt me forever, a face dominated by hooded eyes whose tears were distillations of the sorrows of the world, eyes that delighted and appalled me since, in their luminous and perplexed depths, I saw all the desolation of America, or of more than that – of all estrangement, our loneliness, our abandonment. Our Lady of the Sorrows, her face whiter than her shroud, offered her unmerciful captor a tribute of the concentrate of all the tears that had been shed in red-plush fleapits on five continents over the sufferings she had mimicked with such persuasiveness they had achieved a more perfect degree of authenticity than any she might have undergone in real life, since half the world had seen those sufferings and found them atrocious enough to weep over. Unless she, all unknowing, had become the focus of their own pain, the receptacle of all the pain they projected out of their own hearts upon her image and so had wept for themselves, though they imagined they wept for Tristessa, and, in this way, had contrived to deposit all the burdens of their hearts upon the frail shoulders of the tragedy queen.

Her name itself whispered rumours of inexpressible sadness; the lingering sibilants rustled like the doomed petticoats of a young girl who is dying.

Now I saw her in her spare and emaciated flesh, she looked far more of a ghost than she had done when, the choc-ice melting in my hand, I sat in childhood cinemas redolent of wet mackintoshes, Jeyes Fluid, stale urine, and watched her – for example – nursing the lepers until she caught the dread disease herself, and the missionary she loved (who had rejected her because she was a fallen woman) married her as soon as it was too late. She wore a veil thick enough to hide the ravages of the disease at the ceremony but they could not touch, of course. So she died and he was sorry and so was I; I licked the melted chocolate from the silver paper, to extract a bit of comfort from it. So some of my own tears must have glistened in Tristessa's eyes since I had dowered her with such a shower long ago, far away, over the rainbow, when I was a child.

When I was a child, she had not wrung my withers to no purpose, since now she gave me my tears back again with interest.

But Zero could not be moved by tears and dropped a mouthful of hot, thick curses on the ambiguous woman who was like nothing so much as her own shadow, worn away to its present state of tangible insubstantiality because, perhaps, so many layers of appearances had been stripped from it by the camera – as if the camera had stolen, not the soul, but her body and left behind a presence like an absence that lived, now, only in a quiet, ghostly, hypersensitised world of its own. Even her terror had a curiously stylised quality; she acted it out with absolute conviction but I cannot tell whether or not she experienced it.

I could make no connection between her face and any notion of common humanity. Yet the old bones of beauty stuck with a shock through skin that seemed thinner than rice paper; cadaverous, sepulchral Tristessa, how thin your lips were but how beautifully they curved! What an enormous web of pale hair hung on the air behind you when you moved! Your eyes, with their desolating resonance, were, I remember, stuck all around with sequins. Your mouth was painted with "rose cendre" lipstick. You had doused yourself with Guerlain's "L'Heure Bleu". You were the memory of grief and I fell in love with you the minute I saw you, though I was a woman and you were a woman and, at a conservative estimate, old enough to be my mother.

All the harem had climbed up to the crows' nest by now but it could not hold them all so they clustered in the doorway, giggling and flashing their torches this way and that way so the light came and went like an affliction of the eyes. Zero roughly dragged her to her knees and would have stripped away her négligé then and there to show the girls how she looked when she was naked if, with a sudden access of amazing dignity suited to an audience of millions, she had not commanded him to let her go with a gesture of such authority Zero fell back, although he laughed ironically at her as he did so.

So she got to her feet by herself, drawing the flying panels of chiffon around her somewhat proudly. She was taller than I'd ever dreamed – more than six feet tall; they had had to stand her co-stars on orange boxes so that she did not tower over them. The rushing wind took hold of her hair and dragged it out to all its amazing length; it was nearly as long as she was and white as bone. Once she had attained an upright position, the wind seemed to tautly maintain her in it; the elements conspired in her defiance of us but all the girls went on laughing and Zero let her alone, although he kept within a wary distance of her in case she came out of her dream long enough to pitch herself over the glass precipice and so escape him.

Touchingly, now she tries to put herself to rights; she has decided she is receiving visitors – what else can have happened? Or perhaps she suspects we have been sent from Central Casting and she must put her best profile forward for an invisible director. She dabs her moist eyelids with the hem of her négligé and puts her hands up to the bewildering breakers of her hair before she turns on her visitors that face of an exquisite corpse and, after a still moment of blindness, allows a gracious smile to flicker at the corners of her mouth. And speaks.

"Welcome," she says, "to Juliet's tomb. How charming of you all to come, on such a very dark night! And I thought there were no more parties! Forgive me if I seemed inhospitable, at first; my seclusion . . . a silly reluctance to meet strangers. . ."

Her voice is soft and a little faded, as if it had been locked away in scented cachets in her throat all these years. And the harem's giggling becomes random and sporadic, becomes crisped with, yes, fear.

Then she advanced upon the cluster of girls in the doorway and, one by one, she began to shake their hands with a preposterously regal condescension, proud as a martyred queen on that confined catwalk high in the air at the tip of the swaying house. And this air of majesty was so impressive, her conviction of authority so convincing, that Emmeline even tried to bob down in a gross facsimile of a curtsey, all cramped at the top of the stair as she was, and Tiny muttered, though God knows where she'd picked up the phrase: "Madame . . ." while Apple Pie was too intimidated to do anything but duck her head and blush. I stood beside Zero on the parapet and heard his sardonic chuckle at this little comedy until she had shaken every hesitantly proffered hand and turned to us. When her cold, white hand folded round mine like the toothed mouth of a bloodless animal, I managed to stammer out just a little of my admiration.

"Always a fan, since childhood, Tristessa. Your *Wuthering Heights*, I thought my heart would break . . . Tristessa, Tristessa."

"You enchanting child," she responds. Her eyes clear for an instant and direct their dark regard into my own. Pallor, shallow breathing, a prickle of cold sweat – I want to fall; I must not fall into the chasms of her eyes where I see myself reflected twice, my golden hair whipped by the wind to foam, the soft, bruisable flesh of my innocent face an invitation to the marauder just as the ripe peach invites teeth. For the most fleeting instant, this ghostly and magnetic woman challenges me in the most overt and explicit manner. The abyss on which her eyes open, ah! it is the abyss of myself, of emptiness, of inward void. I, she, we are outside history. We are beings without a history, we are mysteriously twinned by our synthetic life.

With her glance like a beam of black light, she ordered me to negate myself with her. It was the most imperious demand for submission I could ever have imagined. I felt a sensation within me as though the neck of my new womb moved. I caught hold of the glass parapet to prevent myself falling.

Zero was roused to fury and spat in her face.

"Dyke!"

Tristessa dropped her eyes at once and shuddered.

The wind blew a fold of chiffon over her face and
hid it. But Zero thrust the muzzle of his gun into her
back and forced her down the spiral staircase while
the troupe of girls followed them. I hung back;
I stayed alone for a moment in the quick, dark
night. Below me, in spreading, concentric circles,
like those a fish makes when it rises in still water,
spun round the lower tiers; above me arched the
black sky pierced by the gas jets of the stars. I felt
a tumultuous exhilaration; I felt that the house was
a glass warship in which we had all embarked on a
desperate expedition to a destination at the heart of
the dark in a nameless zone, where we would find
the key to an unimaginable secret.

They decided to try Tristessa for spreading sterility
and improvised a courthouse out of the gallery where
she kept her statues. On the floor below the floor
below the floor below the crows' nest, in the floor
above the Hall of Immortals, all the apocalyptic
almost-beasts she had formed from liquid glass lay
about the carpetless floor; here were the largest and
most opulently flowing of the fruit-like things she
had cast in her own swimming pool. She stood
among them like their shepherdess and showed
no fear of her visitors at all, no, not a flicker of
apprehension.

The girls had found a store of candles in the
basement and stuck them by their own grease on
to the surfaces of the glass zoo so the little flames
were reflected again and again in the innumerable
reflective planes the room contained and made a
touching show of brightness against the night that

licked round the construction. There was a sweet, ruttish smell in the room mixed with the rank stench of the unwashed tribe of women freshly odorous in the heat of so many candles, the smell of melted wax and the odour of regret which was the special perfume of Tristessa's skin.

When the room was well lit, Zero's wives perched upon the glass beasts or squatted on the floor in a state of hushed expectancy while I crouched as close as I could get to the heroine of the night as she lay on the floor with her arms bound behind her with her own silk scarf. Her face was perfectly impassive; but, now and then, as if briefly visited by feeling, she sobbed a greeting or an invitation to pain. I choked with love and pity for her.

Zero cracked his whip over her and, though the lash did not touch her, her body convulsed in a gigantic wince, though not immediately; after she heard the crack of the whip, she turned slowly to look at Zero and his instrument and *then*, lavishly histrionic, convulsed, although by now he'd coiled his whip away. She was that much in control of her experience. She made her responses in her own good time, with great art – but the girls all laughed uproariously until Zero silenced them with a gesture that indicated he might turn the whip on *them*, if they weren't careful. His single eye now glared with all the intensity of gratified dementia. He was a bull in a china shop; he had come to break things. He set his booted foot on Tristessa's neck and laughed and cracked his whip about him with all the extraversion of a lover of pigs while she lay tragically still, for she was a great actress.

"I am the avenging phallic fire," he informed her. "I've come to fecundate your sterility, you dyke of dykes, you jamjar of infertility."

With that, he ripped away her chiffon négligé to reveal a water-pale torso, a breast as hollow as a hole, a rib-cage like an abacus. The girls cheered while Tristessa writhed and moaned. Beneath her robe she was stark naked but for a g-string sequinned to match her eyes. Zero now beat her a little with the butt of his whip and she rolled about to try to evade the blows but all the same they raised a tracery of cruel red lace upon her arms and sides. When he had beaten her enough to bring out her tears again, he took the knife from his boot, thrust her down with a foot in her belly and slit the g-string with one sweep of his stiletto.

And then, astonished, he lurched back against a great glass and dislodged it from its chrome pedestal so that it fell and shattered on the floor. The girls let out such a loud collective gasp the candle flames shivered; they rose up on their mounts to catch the action better while I involuntarily darted forward and then fell back, covering my eyes, for I could hardly believe what I saw, what the parted strands of silver had revealed.

How Mother would have laughed!

Out of the vestigial garment sprang the rude, red-purple insignia of maleness, the secret core of Tristessa's sorrow, the source of her enigma, of her shame.

His wailing echoed round the gallery of glass as his body arched as if he were attempting to hide herself within himself, to swallow his cock within her thighs; and when I saw how much the heraldic regalia of his sex appalled him, I thought that Mother would say he had become a woman because he had abhorred his most female part – that is, his instrument of mediation between himself and the other.

Zero rose to his knees and gazed with wonder at the spectacle.

"Shee-it!" he exclaimed again and then began to laugh. As if at a signal, the girls all burst out laughing too and slid off the statues to crowd round the poor, bound, female man. Emmeline stretched out her hand to touch the organs that had been the best-kept secret in the whole world while Tiny derisively applied her lips to the open wound that was Tristessa's mouth. Some of the other girls chose their favourite method of desecration, pulled down their dungarees and pissed copiously on the floor, while others tore off every stitch of clothing and danced obscene naked dances in front of him, contemptuously flourishing their fringed holes at him and brandishing mocking buttocks. The clamour and gesticulations were those of the monkey house.

But, unobserved in this mayhem, I crept up to him and kissed her pitiful, bare feet with their fine ankles and high ballerina's arches. I could not think of him as a man; my confusion was perfect – as perfect as the exemplary confusion of the proud, solitary heroine who now underwent the unimaginable ordeal of a

confrontation with the essential aspect of its being
it had so grandly abandoned, the implicit maleness
it had never been able to assimilate into itself.

That was why he had been the perfect man's
woman! He had made himself the shrine of his
own desires, had made of himself the only woman
he could have loved! If a woman is indeed beautiful
only in so far as she incarnates most completely the
secret aspirations of man, no wonder Tristessa had
been able to become the most beautiful woman in
the world, an unbegotten woman who made no
concessions to humanity.

Tristessa, the sensuous fabrication of the mythology of the flea-pits. How could a real woman ever
have been so much a woman as you?

When I saw Tristessa was a man, I felt a great
wonder since I witnessed, as in a revelation, the grand
abstraction of desire in this person who represented
the refined essence of all images of love and the
dream.

While Zero ingeniously tortured you in your
gallery of glass, you must have been in absolute complicity with him. You must have thought
Zero, with his guns and knives and whips and
attendant chorus of cringing slaves, was a man
worth the ironic gift of that female appearance
which was your symbolic autobiography. I read
it at a glance. You had turned yourself into an
object as lucid as the objects you made from glass;
and this object was, itself, an idea. You were
your own portrait, tragic and self-contradictory.
Tristessa had no function in this world except as

an idea of himself; no ontological status, only an iconographic one.

Tristessa, my darling, before the proposition of my body forced you to become the first term of the syllogism, you did not exist at all in any medium of sensible actuality. Yet something that had chosen to call itself "Tristessa", an anti-being that existed only by mearns of a massive effort of will and a huge suppression of fact, now wept and bled, torn from a non-life of intermediate stasis by Zero's rage.

They made ropes from twisted strips of his own négligé and tied him by his wrists from a steel beam, so there he dangled, naked, revealed. Then they rampaged through the house, breaking windows, smashing furniture, smearing excrement on the walls of the tiny projection theatre and making a bonfire of the rolls of films they found in cans in an open safe in the foyer. The bonfire lit up the interior of the house like a storm lantern.

But I stayed by your side, pretending to them I was guarding you in case you tried to escape – pale pretence. I crouched by your side and saw your strained muscles quiver with pain; when I saw how cruelly tight your bonds were, I stretched out my hand and touched yours. You turned your face towards me and saw my distress. Then you smiled, but said nothing. Blood was caked at the corners of your mouth.

What did Tristessa eat? In the kitchen in the basement, no larger than the galley of a yacht, they found only many tins of a powder that could be converted into a liquid diet by means of the

addition of water; glass jar after glass jar of vitamin
pills; phial upon phial of drugs to make you sleep,
drugs to wake you, drugs to procure hallucinations
for you. In a cupboard were a number of packets
of noodles and a plastic pail in which beansprouts
were growing but these must have been the food
the Oriental deaf-mute, now defunct, ate. Since
the girls found nothing that tempted their own
palates, they poured the contents of the tins down
the sink and pelted one another with vitamin pills
and barbiturates, although they gobbled down the
other drugs in handfuls, sniffed some and injected
themselves with others, using the plastic syringes
they found in cardboard boxes beneath the sink.
Then they smashed all the crockery, turned on all
the taps and left the kitchen just as they wished to
find it. But then they went down yet another hole
in the ground and found a well-stocked wine-cellar.
They broke the tops off the bottles, for they had not
the patience to search for a corkscrew, and soon an
atmosphere of bacchanalia overtook the rout.

They found a mirrored dressing-room – the glass
walls silvered on the outside, so the whole room
was a perfect mirror – where, on a series of racks,
hung the relics of forty years of travesty, gowns
from her roles, furs, crinolines, dresses in which
to receive Academy Awards etc etc etc, clothes for
tennis and golf (poor Tristessa! – but these were
hardly worn at all), for riding, for nightclubbing,
for all the occupations at which a star must be
photographed. Lamé, lace, satin, silk – a room
devoted to disguises and, when Zero gave them

permission (though not before) the girls who were
not already naked snatched off their dungarees and,
eager as children, began to dress up.

Emmeline found the square-necked dress of black
velvet in which Tristessa, as Mary, Queen of Scots,
had been decapitated; it was far too long for her
so she hacked two feet off the skirt in order to
flit about in comfort. Betty Louella put on the
mauve flounces of the camelia lady and discovered
a flowered hat that matched them, while Tiny rooted
out Carmen's scarlet hooped skirt and wound her
black mantilla round and round her head. Sadie and
Emmeline hooked and eyed themselves into fantasies
of gold net and star-dust dating from God knows
what benighted attempt to insert Tristessa into a
musical. While they were dressing themselves up,
so absorbed in the task did they grow they became
quiet hushed and silent – good children, good girls;
but soon the bacchic frenzy gripped them again.

Then they attacked the racks of clothes like beasts.
They tore flowers, ribbons and knots of lace from
gowns they ripped carelessly from the hangers
and pinned these additions to their garments in a
random and antic fashion, to make themselves more
beautiful. Then they savaged the dressing table. They
opened and spilled all the jars of cosmetics, scattering
thick clouds of powder around them and leaving
palm and fingerprints of rouge on the door and
all over the mirror walls, where Marijane drew a
crude picture of Tristessa in lipstick, with all her
hair and a hard-on worthy of Priapus. Inspired by
this, they all seized lipsticks and scrawled obscenities

over every surface of glass. They doused one another
with perfumes and then hurled the empty bottles
through the walls, so the wind came roaring in.
They painted huge circles of mascara round their
eyes and dribbled the black stain over the heaps of
rags to which they had reduced the wardrobe.

When they were as gorgeous as they could make
themselves, all the appurtenances of femininity
with which Tristessa had surrounded himself were
destroyed and they trooped out of the dressing-room
as gaudy as parrots, as odorous as a brothel, cawing
and screeching at the tops of their voices at the
wonders they had achieved.

But I stayed below in the candlelight until Zero
whistled for me and then I had to run. He had been
rooting diligently in a closet and there had found a
neat, dark, evening suit, tails and a white tie, all
complete, even a top hat. Of course – CHOPIN! and
poor Tristessa quite miscast as George Sand, moping
and mewing about as she chewed with distaste on her
cigar and gazed with ill-concealed envy at Ty Power
when he began to cough into his handkerchief and
so usurp her suffering. Zero flourished this suit,
crowing with satisfaction; he ordered me to undress
myself and I climbed into it.

The trousers, of course, were far too long. Off
came six inches with his knife. Then he knotted my
bow tie for me and tipped my topper at a jaunty angle
on my golden head. He stepped back to look at me.
I saw him step back and I saw his reflection in the
mirror step back and the reflection of that reflection
in another mirror stepped back; an entire audience

composed of Zero applauded the transformation that
an endless sequence of reflections showed me was
a double drag. This young buck, this Baudelairean
dandy so elegant and trim in his evening clothes –
it seemed, at first glance, I had become my old self
again in the inverted world of the mirrors. But this
masquerade was more than skin deep. Under the
mask of maleness I wore another mask of femaleness
but a mask that now I never would be able to
remove, no matter how hard I tried, although I
was a boy disguised as a girl and now disguised
as a boy again, like Rosalind in Elizabethan Arden.
In the desert, we played out an arid pastoral.

I only mimicked what I had been; I did not become
it. But I understood immediately that Zero intended
to close the performance with a marriage, the formal
conclusion of pastorals.

He seized the ivory handled powder-puff and
brushed my face with white powder that made me
sneeze and spilled over my shoulders like dandruff.
Then he took a rabbit's foot she must have kept
as a good-luck piece and daubed my cheeks with
rouge, until my face had the bi-coloured anonymity
of Pierrot. The girls left off their play to come
and crouch around him, admiring him for what
he did to me.

Betty Boop had been burrowing among the clothes,
too, and now emerged from the depths of the racks
dragging behind her yard upon yard of white satin,
beaded with seed pearls; Betty Louella pulled down
a box from a shelf that spilled open to let out
six feet of foam, a tulle veil. And Tiny, tittering,

discovered a garland of pearls and orange blossom
under a glass dome.

Then they began preparations for the wedding.

They tied Tristessa's arms behind his back and
dragged him by the hair, bouncing round and round
the spiral staircase, to his own dressing-room where
they gave him a white and red maquillage just like
mine before they forced his unresisting limbs into
the white satin bridal gown he'd last worn thirty
years before in, God help me, coming events . . .
that dreadful marriage scene in *Wuthering Heights*.
Betty Boop had been a hairdresser's apprentice in
another lifetime in Kansas City: she found a brush
and comb and box of tortoiseshell pins. She attacked
Tristessa's errant fleece energetically and laughed
when she tugged a tangle so sharply Tristessa cried
out: they showed him no consideration. All the girls
now seated themselves about the room and watched,
with many insults and hurled obscenities, the robing
of the bride.

Yet, slowly, the ritual took possession of them
all as the restoration of beauty took possession of
Tristessa and Betty Boop's fingers insensibly gentled
as, in the mirror, Tristessa saw the grudging hands of
his tormentor were building up again the spectacular
fiction of his beauty. He began, by miraculous
degrees, to grow back into his reflected self. He
was his own souvenir of an immediate reality that
was not one whit the less affecting because it did
not exist. When he was dressed and ready for
whatever humiliations Zero might now devise, with
the white hair coiled on his head, the bones of that

face instructed the crude cosmetics which covered
them to create a formal pattern that seemed to me
an enhancement, since an abstraction, of nature.
He leaned forward and scrutinised the romantic
apparition in the mirror with eyes filled with an
obscure distress and also a luminous pride.

"Isn't it *every* girl's dream to be married in
white?" the virgin bride demanded rhetorically of
the company in her heroic irony; but Zero sneered
and thrashed him briefly about the shoulders with
the handle of his whip so the spell was broken.

The harem pelted him with lipsticks, rouge pots
and eye paint until his satin skirts were daubed and
streaked. Then, jeering, Zero took his arm in a grip
like a vice and half led, half dragged him down the
staircase to the Hall of the Immortals, where we
would be married, and I walked behind, carrying
my silk hat.

Tristessa's glass bed would be our altar. Betty
Boop lit two candles and placed them at either end
of it. The centrifuge of the building whirled the
dismembered waxworks round the floor but the
girls hurried to gather the limbs together and prop
them willy-nilly in rows facing the make-shift altar,
so we should have witnesses and a congregation. But
they put the figures together haphazardly, so Ramon
Navarro's head was perched on Jean Harlow's torso
and had one arm from John Barrymore Junior, the
other from Marilyn Monroe and legs from yet other
donors – all assembled in haste, so they looked like
picture-puzzles.

Tristessa, shaken now and then by shudders, as

though he were in the grip of a bad dream, hid
behind his veil in a corner and I, submitting wholly
to this charade, waited in a lapse of consciousness,
almost as far from life as the waxworks, for the
next pousse of this delirium. The house shuddered
on its circular progression, inscrutable as the world:
Tchaikovsky's strings had been almost ground off
the surface of the record that still, with a rhythmic
hiss, susurrated through the building. The harem
were all to be our bridesmaids and Zero himself
would marry us; he draped himself in a bearskin
from the foyer, pulled the mask down over his head
roaring away.

When the congregation was seated and the girls in
their many-coloured rags had assembled themselves
in a tittering coven behind Tristessa, Zero took his
place before the altar and motioned me to approach.
Cain, the lurcher, trotted beside me as best man but
Tristessa stood still as a stone, he showed no sign
of motion so all the girls gave him a mighty push
and he stumbled down the tumbling room and fell
to his knees before Zero in a foam of tulle. I knelt
blankly before his fabulous, blind profile and Zero
joined our hands.

Zero in his furs was the captain of the glass ship;
after roaring and baying and running through his
full repertory of animal noises he consented, to my
astonishment, to speak. He made an exception to his
rule of non-language to demand of me if I took the
woman in matrimony. Though my throat was so dry
hardly a sound came out, I coughed and strained and
at last, haltingly, said: "Yes." But Tristessa was far

away when he asked him whether or not he would take me; he had left behind him before the altar only his silent envelope and Zero had to kick him in the stomach to elicit a muffled response that could have been a cry of pain rather than an affirmation. Then I had to slip a ring on to his finger so I pulled off the wedding ring Zero had given me when I was married and used that; nothing else was available.

So he made us man and wife although it was a double wedding – both were the bride, both the groom in this ceremony.

Then, at Zero's command, I rose up on tiptoe to kiss him on the mouth. He neither moved nor spoke, it was like kissing a dead person, while the harem pelted us with torn-up scripts. But his eyes gleamed like wet stones; there was a kind of horror in my passion, for you were too close a friend of death for comfort. Ancient terrors rushed into my heart at that shattering moment when I put my lips against your lips. I entered the realm of negation when I married you with my own wedding ring. You and I, who inhabited false shapes, who appeared to one another doubly masked, like an ultimate mystification, were unknown even to ourselves. Circumstances had forced us both out of the selves into which we had been born and now we were no longer human – the false universals of myth transformed us, now we cast longer shadows than a man does, we were beings composed of echoes. These echoes doom us to love. My bride will become my child's father.

(Mother laughed until her fat, black sides shook.)

Zero laughed so much when the happy couple

kissed he lost the balance he precariously kept
upon his wooden leg and tumbled over backwards,
letting rip a resounding fart as he did so. Cain,
full of obscure, canine merriment, jumped about,
barking. But now it was time to bed us and the
harem clustered freshly round, denuding us of the
last scraps of our clothed dignity. Betty Boop and
Tiny took my topper and played football with it
up and down the rows of waxworks while Marijane
tore off Tristessa's floral wreath and dishevelled his
chignon completely. Zero himself took his knife and
sliced the bridal satin into rashers. The immaterial
veil floated to the ground. When I was bare and
could see my youth and beauty dimly reflected in
the whirling walls beyond which the night sky was
now luminously streaked with scarlet, my courage
failed me and I made for the door.

But Zero forestalled me. The whip cracked and
the lash coiled round my ankle, bringing me to the
floor. I was dragged back to the bed, protesting, and
Marijane and Sadie prepared me for the sacrifice.
They grasped my arms firmly while Betty Boop
and Emmeline took hold each one of my ankles
and spread my legs wide, so that the moist, crimson
velvet with which I had been so scrupulously lined
was exhibited to them all like meat.

Now all bayed for Tristessa to mount me.

Tiny and Apple Pie had grasped his arms, though
he showed no signs of running away herself, he was
too dazed. At a sign from Zero, who sat lording it
on the lid of James Dean's coffin with his bearskin
wrapped around him like a Highlander's plaid, Betty

Louella dropped to her knees before Tristessa and applied her intelligent mouth to the cock that seemed to them such a significantly male appendage. At that wet touch, Tristessa started and cried out.

To the East, three times a minute, I saw a brightening of the sky that hinted the sun was about to rise.

Tristessa stared down in amazement at the erection Betty Louella had procured for him. But still he kept perfectly silent; still he said nothing, while they jeered, and Tiny and Apple Pie led him to the bed on which I lay. Zero gave him a great kick in the arse so that, taken by surprise, he lost balance and toppled on top of me so unexpectedly he shook all the breath out of me. The glass bed was cold, hard and exposed as the mountain top on which Abraham presented Isaac with his knife. Now Tristessa, who lay upon me, raised himself upon his arms and gazed into my face. Again, the dark light of his eyes. He spoke; that rustling whisper, the dead leaves of his voice.

"I thought," he said, "I was immune to rape. I thought that I had become inviolable, like glass, and could only be broken."

I felt his cock pressing against my upper thigh; it was quite stiff.

"Passivity," he said. "Inaction. That time should not act upon me, that I should not die. So I was seduced by the notion of a woman's being, which is negativity. Passivity, the absence of being. To be everything and nothing. To be a pane the sun shines through."

Then the sun broke free of the horizon and speared
the room through with a single shaft of brilliance. I
was tired of waiting. I clasped my legs about him
and drew him into me. He came immediately, amidst
the roars of vile applause, and withdrew in almost
the same motion. He tumbled out on to the floor,
uttering great cries, while I writhed on the hard
bed, consumed by unsatisfied desire.

So our marriage was consummated.

So my womanhood was ratified.

Now they flung the wedding veil over Tristessa
and stifled his convulsions as in a butterfly net.
They made a big bundle of the net and hung it
from a hook in the glass roof; every moment, the
gallery filled with more light. Trapped within the
net, Tristessa struggled at first but Zero directed
his gun at him and he grew quiet. Then the girls
flung the heads and limbs of the waxworks about
the room: they dispersed the congregation. Cain
leapt excitedly about.

I got off the bed and looked for some rag to
cover my nakedness because I had grown suddenly
ashamed of it but, before I could find anything, Zero
flung me to the floor and took me from the rear,
in the anal orifice, with extraordinary brutality, to
show me how much he despised me, the pig lover.
In the midst of my pain, I heard Tristessa remonstrate
with him at my treatment. Tristessa? I could hardly
believe my ears! How had he been precipitated into
awareness? But his gentle pleas only made Zero
thrust still harder at the inadequate orifice while
the entire harem cheered.

Then they left me, bleeding and weeping as I was, to complete the destruction of the house. Only the lurcher stayed behind, to guard us. I sat up and dried my eyes with a sliver of white satin I found on the floor. The house echoed with the sound of shattering glass. Above my head, in the cocoon of tulle, Tristessa now spoke; the sleeper was awake at last.

"Free me," he said in his unused voice of a revenant. "Free me and we shall run away together."

What else was there to be done?

"The dog – "

For its red eyes were fixed upon me. Then I saw, fallen from a broken window, a jagged splinter of glass with a point sharp enough to pierce a heart or sever an artery. Slowly, slowly, so as not to startle the dog nor attract his attention nor make him bark, I inched my fingers towards the improvised weapon. Once I held it in my hand, the rest was easy. I whistled to the beast: it loped towards me and I distracted its attention by tickling its ears and kissing its muzzle while I plunged the blade of glass into its throat. It gave a gurgling choke, kicked its hind legs once in the air and fell lifeless from my arms to the floor.

I pulled a coffin across the floor and stood on it in order to carve an opening in Tristessa's net with the sword I'd stabbed the dog with. He stepped down beside me, strange, vague, wondering. I held out my hand to him and he took it.

"What is your name?" he asked me.

"Eve," I said. "Eva."

"Where do you come from?"

"From Beulah. Hurry!"

We darted down the spiral staircase and I would have run out of the house immediately but he motioned me to pause; he had a little further business within it. In the control room in the viscera of the mansion, he sobbed to see the mortal remains of the houseboy that littered the floor but turned swiftly to the panel of dials and selected a switch. Even as we ran back to the lounge, the house began to gain momentum. The bearskins on the floor rose up and sped round; the broken windows caved in with a crash.

We jumped from the verandah and tumbled head over heels on the overgrown lawn. I saw Tristessa had cut his foot on the broken glass and, as we ran towards the helicopter, he left behind him a dabbled track of blood.

The air was full of flying glass and shattered furniture; the house was now spinning so fast the stagnant waters of the pool reflected only a glittering blurr. Tristessa looked back and halted, as if tranced. He would not move, however hard I tugged his hand. He was like Lot's wife.

Cacophany. Above the mechanical clatter of the dissolution of the bizarre edifice, I could hear the terrified screeching of Zero and his harem; as the house whirled past, I saw them clinging helplessly to what spars of metal remained. The artificial gale tore their clothes from them and tossed them lightly sailing on to the desert air. As we watched, one of the girls – I think it was Tiny, she looked so little – gave up the struggle against the maelstrom and let go, to follow the passage of the black velvet dress of which the wind had stripped her. Up it went, the wing of black velvet, unfurled like the black flag of freedom and despair, the black flag of the victory of the spirit . . . in its catastrophe, Tristessa's palace triumphed over its desecrators; up and away, the huge black flag – and there goes Tiny, upwards and outwards she was hurled. She described a despairing trajectory across the morning, to disappear somewhere far away, beyond the walls, driven deep into the sand by the impetus of her own fall.

Now, one by one, all my poor girls began to let go as their strength failed, their arms weakened. Their screams were like broken arches. The house tossed them into the air like clay pigeons; first they swooped, then they dropped. I took Tristessa's arm and pulled at him for we were in great danger from flying debris but he gazed on, transfixed by the grand immolation of the tower of glass he had built in his own image. He was as indifferent to the proximity of the cataclysm as if his beauty must protect him.

Zero still clung to the frame of steel, although all the glass was gone. His arms were clenched round the central pillar, the staircase itself, and now he was quite naked. You could see the harness of leather straps that kept his wooden leg in place. His face was contorted in outrage. Round and round and round, he went, and now the house began to keel over.

The spiral metal core was giving way under the strain, the speed; it tilted like the tower of Pisa and then, with an immense rending, turning, now, more slowly, the tapering spiral began to bend downwards towards the pool as if it were thirsty and wanted to drink. Objects, waxen limbs, chairs, chunks of glass, all that remained within the rib-cage, slithered down into the water: the splashing drenched us. Then, with an immense, jarring shudder, the mechanism that drove the house now gave up the ghost.

It halted with a horrid shock as the metal roots that had driven deep into the earth came out of the ground as easily as radishes when the concrete base itself tore up from the earth and tipped upon its side.

Zero now began to clamber up the central pole of the staircase hand over hand. Perhaps he thought he would be able to jump to safety when it bowed near the ground. But, once the base had tilted far enough, its own weight made the fall inevitable. There was a mighty, tinkling, splashing crash as the denuded frame of steel plunged directly into the waters of the pool, sucking Zero the poet down, down with it, raising a dithering wave that broke upon our heads and streamed down our faces and tried to tug us after it as it swilled back towards its source.

Then there was an immense silence.

Tristessa passed his long hands over his face as if he were rubbing his eyes and looked down with a blank face at his own maleness as if he had never seen it before. He seemed numbed by the rediscovery of his virility; it was incomprehensible to him.

"At first," he said, "I used to conceal my genitals in my anus. I would fix them in position with Scotch tape, so that my mound was smooth as a young girl's. But when the years passed and my disguise became my nature, I no longer troubled myself with these subterfuges. Once the essence was achieved, the appearance could take care of itself."

The early sunlight cast his thin, agonised shadow across the rubble-strewn weeds of the overgrown garden. Now I could see the neglected park in which he had built his home, I saw it was filled with soft, lush trees and plants, bushes of hibiscus, iridescent lilies, orchids green as decay; the Oriental deaf-mute must have watered them daily, with a hose fed at the pool, though he must have spilled a good deal of water because all was tumultuously choked with rank, arid weeds so the beautiful vegetation was engaged in a harsh, continuous struggle to live and now, since there was nobody left to water it, would soon wither for lack of nourishment and die. The quick time of this continent would subdue the waterlogged wreck of the house with the spiral staircase and turn it, before our child quickened in my belly, into a ruin with the air of pre-history about it. Who could have lived here? What giants built it?

As Tristessa, sunk in reverie, gazed at the drowning pool, small items of furnishings now floated to the surface of the once-tranquil water – a bearskin rug; the chrome superstructure of a coffee table; discs that held frozen music; a severed limb or two of an Immortal, limbs dismemberment rendered permanently anonymous . . . arms and legs that might have belonged to anyone. A golden torso bobbed up and floated, pointing its strawberry nipples bravely to the sky, though who could tell who she had been. The lid of a glass coffin, containing a mass of wax roses. And a head, streaked with its own sodden, yellow hair and fearfully patched with scum and weed. The nose had been broken off, one of the blue eyes had dropped out of the socket but the face was still split in a perpetual smile.

Then the strangest item of all the grotesque debris swam up through the refuse; it was Zero's wooden leg.

I shook Tristessa briskly to rouse him. He turned his lycanthropic eyes upon me, which made me shiver.

"I have already forgotten your name and where you come from," he said.

"They call me Eve," I told him. "I was born in Beulah."

"I bore a daughter, once," said Tristessa from the depths of a tranced hallucination. "If she had lived, she would have been just your age. But she was eaten by rats. You must understand, Eva, even if I have forgotten everything, that I understand everything. I know everything because, you see, I can read tears. They map our destiny when they flow down the face. I perform divinations by means of tears, I let my glass flow the same way, at random, in sorrow. I let the glass form the patterns of my tears and then I consult the augury and make my own memorials."

So I understood he was quite mad.

I led him to the helicopter and settled him behind

me on the cushions, among the furs. The machine
coughed and rose into the burnished air while my
passenger gazed from the window at the ruins of his
house with the mild air of a spectator, a witness. So
he, she was lifted as on a wire, the mimic flight of
the theatre, from the tomb she'd made for herself; he
looked about him with the curiosity of Lazarus. The
morning sky of the wintry desert was as white as if
it had been floured. Both our faces were still thickly
rouged and powdered. We were alone together and
had been married.

"Tell me about your childhood," he said to
me, comfortably enough. The park diminished to
vanishing point and the rocky spine behind it dwin-
dled to a dark line across the trackless sand.

I was very much preoccupied with flying the
rattling helicopter, for it staggered and wheezed and
the engine did not respond well to my handling; it
was an unwilling horse. Besides, how could I reply?
That I had been born out of discarded flesh, induced
to a new life by means of cunning hypodermics,
that my pretty face had been constructed out of a
painful fabric of skin from my old inner thighs? So
I gave him only an uncommunicative grunt and he
soon forgot he'd spoken. He settled back among
the cushions and looked out of the window with
a gentle contentment.

He, she – neither will do for you, Tristessa, the
fabulous beast, magnificent, immaculate, composed
of light. The unicorn in a glass wood, beside a
transforming lake. You produced your own symbolism with the diligence of a computer; you had

subjected yourself to such an arid metamorphosis –
the desert, the continent assimilated to the irrational
and absurd beauty of this living creature locked in
her glass mansion, like an allegory of chastity in a
medieval romance.

"For hours, for days, for years, she had wandered
endlessly within herself but never met anybody,
nobody," said Tristessa. "She had given herself to
the world in her entirety and then found nothing
was left; I was bankrupt. She left me for dead and
I covered myself from the cold wind of solitude
with her rags. So wore out an endless time. She
who has been so beautiful consumed me. Solitude
and melancholy, that is a woman's life."

The helicopter fell down suddenly twenty feet; we
dropped like a plummet but I thrust at the stick and
the engine roared, the machine righted itself.

"I dowered lechery with every orifice – I wanted
to be a whore, a cheap one, I sold myself for ten
cents a time in the meanest bars, where sputum
mixed with blood and sperm in the sawdust. On
the Barbary Coast, they put oilcloth on the beds
so the men won't tear the sheets when their boot
heels jerk. Degradation is the subtlest drug, the most
insinuating. But they could do nothing to me I had
not already imagined. The rats ate my baby and did
not even leave the bones behind."

What was he wailing for – regret that these things
had *not* happened to him and he could only imagine
them? For all he'd been had been the greatest female
impersonator in the world, and so forever cheated
of experience.

How much he must have both loved and hated women, to let Tristessa be so beautiful and make her suffer so!

I never knew his real name, nor why he had chosen to perform such a violent operation upon himself. I don't know who else might have been in on the gross deception, what movie moguls, what make-up artists, what drama coaches – who had sealed their lips at this ironic joke played on the world? (What a satire Tristessa had been upon romanticism!)

I remember publicity had claimed she was of French-Canadian extraction, because of her name, St Ange. So I tried him with some words of French but he looked blank. His hair floated like that of a seer; his kisses were cold and chilled me. All I had known decomposed in the arctic of your embrace – whiteness, silence. He kissed my cunt with infinite tenderness and said, with soft, sweet surprise: "Who would have thought such a little hole could give so much pleasure!" He was a mad, old man with long, white hair like Ezekiel.

Now it was midday and the sun stood directly overhead. The moving shadow of the helicopter sped more quickly than we did over a terrain that grew increasingly barbarous. Behind us lay the wind-dimpled reaches of fine sand, before us a rampart of rocks yet nowhere did we perceive any sign of habitation, of life. The engine now began to retch ominously, we must be running out of petrol. There was nothing for it but to cast ourselves on the merciless breast of this inverted ocean, where only the specks of mica glittered, where we should soon die together.

The machine bumped down into a soft bed, spraying a fine, pale powder over the windows, and came to a halt. My companion uttered a wild cry and leapt from the cabin. He ran a few paces in the yielding sand, then flung back his head and raised his arms to heaven in the attitude of an Old Testament prophet interceding with his maker. The sun blazed in the ends of his hair and ripped through his translucent skin. He addressed sky and silence as though certain of an answer.

While he continued to wait, I set to and made a little shelter from the sun, stretching some of Zero's Indian coverlets out on the opened doors of the helicopter and piling cushions below them until I'd made a blue corner of shade. My lips were already cracking with thirst and there was nothing to drink. To think we might be dead by morning gave me an exquisite erotic shudder. I called to Tristessa but he was praying and did not hear me so I lay down on the cushions to wait for him.

The dry heat attacked my throat and the insides of my nostrils cruelly. I could scarcely breathe. My heart was pounding so fiercely I could move only with a deathly lassitude. I looked down at my slow limbs; they were already dusted with sand, like a fine, golden powder and I thought, how delicious I look! I look like a gingerbread woman. Eat me. Consume me.

Here we were at the beginning or end of the world and I, in my sumptuous flesh, was in myself the fruit of the tree of knowledge: knowledge had made me, I was a man-made masterpiece of skin and bone, the technological Eve in person.

I saw myself. I delighted me. I reached out my hand and touched my own foot in a sudden ecstasy of narcissistic gratification at its delicacy and littleness. I drew my discoverer's hand along the taut line of my shin and my thigh. My yellow hair spilled out over the cushion in voluptuous disarray. I remember that cushion; it was covered in red, yellow and blue Indian cotton sewn with little discs of mirror that gave it a tinkling look. And there was another cushion with a brown and black paisley print. And another Amerindian hand-woven abstraction. And a fourth made out of an enormous American flag (the stars and stripes forever). All the cushions, stained with food and drink and dribbling and crusted sexual moistures, all filthy, all faintly, mustily redolent of old incense and pot. The sun shone through the weft and warp of the cotton roof, making of the patterns of flowers upon it areas of deeper darkness in its reticulated shadow.

A vague shimmer now affected my eyes but I saw Tristessa, after an interminable time, reluctantly acknowledge that no reply would come from the heavens and bow his head in acquiescence as though the silence in itself was a reply.

"Come into the shade," I whispered raucously.

He came towards me. I know who we are; we are Tiresias.

A little startled by, a little apprehensive of the masculine apparatus of which he now found himself

the master, he approached me as warily as the unicorn
in the tapestry at the Musée de Cluny edges towards
the virgin. The sun had slipped past its meridian and
now illuminated him from behind; for a moment,
he seemed to me surrounded in the oblong glory
of light which emanates from divine figures – an
aureole or vessica, celestial limelight. "More stars
than there are in heaven," had been MGM's motto.
This transforming light covered his nakedness like a
garment; no, it was his flesh itself that seemed made
of light, flesh so insubstantial only the phenomenon
of persistence of vision could account for his presence
here. The habit of being a visual fallacy was too
strong for him to break; appearance, only, had
refined itself to become the principle of his life.
He flickered upon the air.

Yet, like the unicorn, he knelt beside me in his
sacral innocence and laid his hallucinated head in
my lap as carefully as if it were not his own but
some fragile borrowing of which he had to take
the greatest care. I felt his cheek on my skin and
that whispering, tenuous mass of hair settle on my
belly like shed feathers of birds, the white wings of
a great, dead bird blown by a gale far inland from
its ocean, the veritable, Baudelairean albatross. But
the whiteness of his hair contained within it every
shade of moony purple, of opalescent green of roseate
pink, and I stretched out my hand and touched his
fleece, I grasped a greedy lover's handful of his fleece
and drew his head to my breasts. I experienced a
mysterious contraction of the nerves.

He licked my right nipple, a unicorn at a salt lick,

and covered my other breast with his left hand. I felt the sand with which I was powdered irritate deliciously under his touch. I was now half-fainting with longing but I was scared to make any sharp, explicit, unexpected movement in case I frightened him away and he darted off across the wastes on his long, crane's legs, so I only sighed a little, to show pleasure. He softly bit at my right nipple and began to laugh at the back of his throat, for now he was growing potent; I caught his cock between my thighs and squeezed it, but lightly – I didn't want him to come so quickly, I wanted time, I wanted the swooning, dissolvent woman's pleasure I had, heretofore, seen but never experienced. With his free hand, he now began to explore the raw, exquisite, violet oyster Holy Mother had inserted in the russet gash that ran over with viscosity and twitched uncontrollably.

He and I, she and he, are the sole oasis in this desert.

Flesh is a function of enchantment. It uncreates the world.

He told me my intimacy smelled of cheese, no – not quite like cheese . . . and rummaged in a forgotten word-hoard of metaphor but at last was forced to abandon imagery, since it was inadequate, and he could only say it was a sweetish smell, but rotten, too, and also a little salty . . . the primordial marine smell, as if we carry within us the ocean where, at the dawn of time, we were all born. This wild, rank, acrid odour hung about us; the smell of the first sea, that covered everything, the waters of beginning.

Speech evades language. How can I find words the equivalent of this mute speech of flesh as we folded ourselves within a single self in the desert, under our dappled canopy, on our bed of filthy cushions? Alone, quite alone, in the heart of that gigantic metaphor for sterility, where our child was conceived on the star-spangled banner, yet we peopled this immemorial loneliness with all we had been, or might be, or had dreamed of being, or had thought we were – every modulation of the selves we now projected upon each other's flesh, selves – aspects of being, ideas – that seemed, during our embraces, to be the very essence of our selves; the concentrated essence of being, as if, out of these fathomless kisses and our interpenetrating, undifferentiated sex, we had made the great Platonic hermaphrodite together, the whole and perfect being to which he, with an absurd and touching heroism, had, in his own single self, aspired: we brought into being the being who stops time in the self-created eternity of lovers.

The erotic clock halts all clocks.

Eat me.

Consume me, annihilate me.

When I was a man, I could never have guessed what it would be like to be inside a woman's skin, an outer covering which records with such fidelity, such immediacy, each sensation, however fleeting. His kisses exploded like tracer bullets along my arms. I had lost my body; now it was defined solely by his, yet even then I saw fragments of old movies playing like summer lightning on the lucid planes of his face, the shadow show upon the bare bones beneath – I'd know your skull on Golgotha, Tristessa, although you seem to have a hundred faces, so many moods cross over it so quickly.

We sucked at the water bottle of each other's mouth for there was nothing else to drink. Turn and turn about, now docile, now virile – when you lay below me all that white hair shifted from side to side over Old Glory, your hair dragged your head impetuously with it, this way and that way; I beat down upon you mercilessly, with atavistic relish, but the glass woman I saw beneath me smashed under my passion and the splinters scattered and recomposed themselves into a man who overwhelmed me.

When I was at the point of orgasm, I would find myself moving through a succession of small, panelled, interconnected rooms which appeared to me with all the vividness of actuality, and then they would dematerialise under the stress of those fleshly impressions that require another language, not speech, a notation far less imprecise than speech, to log them. God knows where these suites of rooms came into my head from; they contained brown panelling, lighted candles and, yes, white roses but they were not chapels. Though they seemed to me perfectly familiar, I do not know what they were nor what they meant. As I sobbed out too much pleasure, your body also clenched in the mysterious equivalence of orgasm, that solvent of the self. After that, we would lie still while the sun dried our sweat.

Masculine and feminine are correlatives which

involve one another. I am sure of that – the quality
and its negation are locked in necessity. But what
the nature of masculine and the nature of feminine
might be, whether they involve male and female,
if they have anything to do with Tristessa's so
long neglected apparatus or my own factory fresh
incision and engine-turned breasts, that I do not
know. Though I have been both man and woman,
still I do not know the answer to these questions.
Still they bewilder me.

I have not reached the end of the maze yet. I
descend lower, descend lower. I must go further.

The lateral beams of the setting sun melted the
gold; it turned to alchemical gold. Our love could
sustain us no longer for we were too hungry, too
thirsty, too raw and sore to take more joy in it.
We had not finished with one another – I was a
woman and therefore insatiable, he was insatiable
as a woman – but excess exhausts itself. The cold
night came and we huddled together in the cabin
of the helicopter in an alloyage of skin.

So many stars! And such moonlight, enough
moonlight to let a regiment of alchemists perform
the ritual of the dissolution of the contents of the
crucible, which, Baroslav, the Czech, had told me,
may only be taken in polarised light, that is, light
reflected from a mirror, or else by moonlight. I
never saw a moon so fat and white and round, a
moon that bleached all the darkness from the sky
so the night looked like the negative of the day, or
else a cool day itself, without colours. The silence
was absolute and the desert so featureless the terrain

now looked as if it were subtly rounded; the world showed us how round it was and we could see every side of the rim of a horizon that looked near enough for us to be able to stretch out our hands and touch it. I drew the furs round Tristessa's shoulders, and when I did so, I covered myself up too, because I lay so close to him. Neither as man nor woman had I understood before the unique consolation of the flesh.

"Perhaps," he said, "there will be a little dew at the end of the night and we will lick it and that will refresh us."

His voice had almost vanished in his parched throat. I was light-headed with thirst and the un-accustomed tempests that had shaken me throughout the endless afternoon. When I looked through the window of the cabin, I thought we were beached on the breast of a pearl, so white and swollen did the sand look and then I thought, perhaps we've landed on one of my own breasts, on my left one. . . Then I remembered my surgery and its perpetrator and tried to laugh, because I'd played such a trick on Mother, had fallen in love. But the sand caught in my throat and the rasping pain when I tried to laugh brought me out of my dream into another, a dream of fur and moonlight and the arms of the beautiful demented one that held me with as much care as if I, too, was a materialisation of the moon.

And the most beautiful thing of all was that we were slowly dying. The desert was drying us up. The desert would mummify us in the iconic and

devastating beauty of our embrace, I nothing but a
bracelet of bright hair around his bones.

Tristessa spoke, although the slow death of
the desert was already at work in his voice.

"I would appear behind a torn curtain while a fat,
black, syphilitic piano player laid down an infinitely
poignant blues. I would wear red gloves, a red mask
and black stockings. First of all, my legs showed
beneath the curtain and they would pound their fists
and glasses on the tables and shriek like banshees for
more, so up the curtain would go, slowly, stripping
me inch by inch, inch by inch by inch, and their
eyes struck me through like arrows while I danced
and they howled like the damned in hell. I was a
lost soul. Tristessa is a lost soul who lodges in me;
she's lived in me so long I can't remember a time
she was not there, she came and took possession of
my mirror one day when I was looking at myself.
She invaded the mirror like an army with banners;
she entered me through my eyes.

"You must keep your eyes closed when you look
at me, Eva."

He stroked my face with fingers that still wore
Tristessa's rings, very, very gently, and I did not
close my eyes for I saw in his face how beautiful I was.

"She had been very little when she wore pigtails,
I remember, and had a little gingham apron with a
piece of gingerbread in the pocket. A bite extracted
from this piece of gingerbread had left behind a
serrated indentation of the teeth which had nibbled
it. Eaten by rats, poor wee thing. It was such an

old house! Immense rooms, so cold, so dark. Her mother was dead; they laid her out in her wedding dress with all the white roses – they covered her bed with white roses, not with camelias, that came later, and so she wandered along the boulevard of broken dreams until she became one herself."

So he described the symbolic schema to which he attached the label, Tristessa; now he hunted her down these corridors of artificial memory, and yet his quarry was the hunter. He had been she; though she had never been a woman, only ever his creation.

"I performed an acrobatic dance in a tent. I paid out a line of self-created gravity towards the beginning and the end and I myself was the taut rope on which I poised on a single toe, raising and letting fall those enormous sleeves of absolute darkness which depended from my arms. My act preceded the dwarfs who wrestled in mud and followed an educated horse who picked out simple tunes with his right front hoof upon a specially constructed piano. In the Klondyke, the miners pelted me with lumps of gold and I thought: 'How glorious it is to be a woman.'"

He suffered terribly from his memories, but he had only invented them to make him suffer. And this fictive autobiography might have had some trace element of fact in it, for all I know, though nothing in it tallied with what I'd seen of Tristessa in all those long-ago, demolished cinemas. As the moon went down, the stars came out. My eyes filled with mirages of lakes and our little boat sailed over this sea of infertility, closer and closer to perpetual absence. Now his fingers unravelled again the seamless texture of the skin of my breasts and belly so that again I opened for him the sluice upon the sea inside me.

"But I, no, I never opened on this kind of chasm, no matter how beautifully I danced nor what death-defying leaps I performed upon my trapeze. I never lodged in a cave like this and never thought such a little mouth could sing such a loud song. . ."

The furs fell away and we embraced upon the snow field in an extremity of fever and desire while the stars flashed and circled over our bewildered heads. When the water-drops dashed in my face, I was not roused; I thought I was still dreaming, it was such a thankfully refreshing fall. A second and a third time water splashed down upon us and I licked the water from Tristessa's skin with my parched tongue. Prismatic raindrops ran together on his eyebrows and spilled down his cheeks, so I thought we were turning into water and would therefore be able to drink freely.

Then a pair of hands in black leather gauntlets grasped Tristessa's shoulders. He was wrenched out of me like a cork from a bottle.

I screamed with disappointment and outrage.

Then another bucket of water was thrown over me as I rolled on my back and that was followed by a blanket, so my shouts were muffled. After a few moments, I came to myself. I lay quite still, dazed with astonishment; outside the momentary safety of the blanket, I could hear the crunch of sharp heels in sand and a voice barking orders.

This voice, in spite of its clipped consonants, breaks, sometimes, on a squeak. It is a masked voice; the orders it gives disguises who it is that gives them. I hear Tristessa's ghostly reprimands but cannot make out what he is saying; I lift a corner of the blanket to peer and instantly a gauntleted hand seizes my wrists and snaps handcuffs on them.

Before they take the blanket away, they make me put on a spare pair of mechanic's overalls they happen to have with them in the jeep, for they cannot bear to see my nakedness.

We are captured.

Tristessa and I, both securely handcuffed, stood at the junction of the beams of the headlights of fifteen jeeps drawn up in a circle around us. He and I were each attended by a non-commissioned officer dressed in drab-green whipcord breeches and a matching, short-sleeved, open-necked shirt in heavy duty cotton, with a peaked hat on his head to distinguish him from the other ranks, who wore forage caps. All had highly polished boots of brown leather and bristled with guns and ammunition belts. They all wore their hair cut en brosse and were as clean as the well-scrubbed pine table in an old-fashioned farm kitchen.

There were perhaps seventy soldiers in this scrupulous militia. They stood at well-disciplined ease and gazed at us with pure, childish eyes of wonder and – yes – distaste. Each one of them wore a crucifix made out of iron around his neck on an iron chair. Not one of them was a day older than thirteen.

Though we were both bound, the strong young arms of the soldiers gripped us tightly, no precaution was overlooked.

Tristessa and I strained towards one another, yearning. They had thrown an officer's greatcoat over him. He looked like Cassandra after the fall of Troy, disaster streaming from his disordered hair.

Then the Colonel of the regiment descended from the jeep where, unseen by us, he had been observing all that had occurred. There was a unanimous click from the heels of their boots as they all sprang at once to attention. Although it was the middle of the night, the Colonel wore dark glasses. He was dressed exactly like his officers with the exception of the shirt for, above the waist, he was entirely naked but for a skilful tattoo, executed in the liveliest colours, that covered his chest entirely. It was a copy of Leonardo's "Last Supper" and his breathing and the rippling of his skin as he walked gave an uncanny appearance of almost-movement to the faces of the Christ and his disciples. The Colonel's boots, besides, were tooled with gold.

He stepped up to us briskly. The officer kicked me so I fell in the sand in an involuntary obeisance, but Tristessa, however much they beat him, obeyed an impulse towards dignity and stayed standing although he swayed dangerously, like a beautiful statue about to fall.

"I am the scourge of Christ," announced the Colonel. His troops cried out together: "Alleluya!"

in shrill, sweet voices. They made a brave noise in the tenantless silence.

"Lechery!" said the Colonel. His voice went up an octave in outrage and broke upon a held note. He was the senior man, he was fourteen. He scrutinised me through his dark glasses, informed me that Christ had forgiven the woman taken in adultery, motioned my officer to give him the key, unfastened my handcuffs, threw them away with a grand gesture and told me to go and sin no more.

But he told Tristessa that the Bible was silent on the subject of the treatment of the man in the case; and, furthermore, an old man such as he ought not to wear his hair so long. He called for a pair of hair-clippers. They beat Tristessa to his knees with the butts of their revolvers and now he began to moan. I had no choice but to impotently witness his distress since two soldiers pinioned me, I could not move. Then the Colonel folded his arms and stood back while the regimental barber clipped off all Tristessa's white hair and then fetched water, a brush and soap, lathered his skull and shaved it quite bare. The night-wind tumbled the soft, pale tresses in the sand, an enormous mound, white as snow – only the roots were yellowish, as if tarnished. Tristessa, kneeling, watched his rippling hairs with a faint surprise.

"I am not Samson," he said in a strangely bland voice. "I have no strength to lose."

One long hand extended to draw the collar of his great-coat around him, to protect himself against their eyes, and the rings upon it flashed, but the

Colonel seized his hands, tore off the jewels and stamped his booted foot upon them, so that the sand spurted up in little puffs, precocious Savanorola that he was. Tristessa stared at his own bare fingers and then at the Colonel's fury. He broke into a perfectly pure and silver laugh. Before my eyes, even though they'd shaved him and scrubbed the white paint from his face, in all his pared-down integrity of a death's head, he changed into his female aspect. He reverted entirely to the sinuous principle of his notion of femininity. With a single, uncoiling motion, he rose up from his knees and pressed his lips to the Colonel's mouth.

The kiss did not last long. The Colonel uttered a sharp cry and started back. His face twisted; he doubled over and vomited copiously in the sand.

An officer shot Tristessa immediately with his revolver. A devastating sorrow overcame me. Then they dug a hole in the sand, threw in his body, this shallow grave the destination of the false goddess, filled in the hole, forced me at gunpoint to the Colonel's jeep and the entire cavalcade drove off over the desert, leaving behind us, like a grave-marker, the abandoned helicopter with its doors dangling from its hinges and the little canopy I'd rigged up flapping forlorn in the fading moonlight.

Ten

They treated me as kindly as they knew how because they thought I had been wronged, they gave me hot coffee from a thermos flask but I refused to drink it, I spat it out and would not say one word to them. I crouched in a corner of the jeep. My teeth chattered: now and then, I moaned. The Colonel sat beside the driver with his arms resolutely folded. When the day dawned, the cavalcade stopped, the militia dismounted, all took towels and, discreetly concealing their private parts while they did so, they changed into shorts and performed a rigorous programme of calisthenics until they were running with sweat.

I saw they had all had their nipples pierced. Dangling from each nipple was a little round medallion made of gold that shone in the sunshine. The medallion on the left nipple was inscribed with the word: GOD and that on the right nipple, with the word: AMERICA.

After they had towelled themselves briskly down, the Colonel led them in prayers for half an hour. His words came to me clearly, where I hid my misery in

the jeep; he prayed for strength and courage to restore
law and order in the godless state of California. He
called upon the God of Battles. Peering over the edge
of the jeep, I saw how he flexed his muscles while
he made his orizens so that the holy heads upon his
chest seemed to nod their heads in approbation. He
looked very stern and noble but the early sun caught
his very fair skin and irritated it to an angry pink
even during the half hour he harangued his men
and I saw his hair was so blond and cropped so
close the skin of the scalp showed through. After
prayers were done, the militia took paraffin stoves
and pans from the jeep and began to cook breakfast.
The delicious smell of frying bacon reminded me of
everyday things and I managed to eat a little from the
tin plate heaped with food they passed me. I sopped
up the sauce from the beans with a hunk of bread
and saw all the soldiers had plenty to eat; they had
brought large stores of cans along with them.

The Colonel sat apart from his men on a folding
canvas chair his batman brought out from the back
of the jeep and set up for him before a neat little
card-table. But he ate the same food as his soldiers,
with a fine display of egalitarian relish, and, when
everyone was finished, led them all in a joyous
grace. They were not soldiers but souldiers. While
they boiled billies of water to wash the dishes, an
officer marched me before the Colonel.

I stood to attention as well as I could, from fear. I
thought how childlike and vulnerable his jaw looked,
how delicate and as yet unformed his mouth; I ceased
to feel afraid of him when I identified my own feeling

of pity and concern for him – heavens! it was maternal. So I guessed he must be, in reality, the very youngest in all his regiment, must lie about his age to impress them and wore those dark glasses all the time to give himself an air of greater maturity. But all the same, they were murderous children, off on their godly escapade.

I had not yet fully understood that Tristessa was dead.

All the time, the boys in green watched the Colonel with so much devotion in their wide, unshadowed eyes it was obvious that every one of them was head over heels in love with him and would have gone through hell, endured the most savage hardships, fought like tigers against overwhelming odds, to win one word of approbation from his pale mouth and earn the shoulder-clap of fellowship from the boy-god of war. They polished their boots for him alone; they scrubbed themselves in cold water to make their bodies more acceptable to him; when their hands absent-mindedly wandered to their tender young cocks during the lonely hours of the nightwatch or in the furry privacy of their sleeping-bags, only the thought of the little blond eagle and his appalling asceticism preserved them from self-pollution. This love they bore him bonded them in a brotherhood that gave them all the look of kin. A common feeling expressed itself in their expressions so all had the same look of mute adoration and hence they all looked the same. He had contrived to instil this hero-worship in them so strongly that it was no longer in the least related to the admirability or otherwise of his actual conduct.

He could vomit at a kiss and they did not think he
was a coward; they thought it was further proof of
purity. There was a thick down on his face, which
gave his skin a wonderfully soft and tender look,
he would have photographed beautifully.

He was the son of a millionaire from Florida who
had made a pile in Vietnam out of, I believe, some
kind of soft drinks concession, and a fifth wife
who had been his nurse in a private sanatorium
specialising in the treatment of alcoholics. The boy's
conviction that he was Jesus Christ was implemented
by his wealth; augmented by the fervid assurances
of a crazy housekeeper, his only companion in the
years of childhood after his parents died together in
a drunken car crash; and the indisputable fact that he
had been born on Christmas Day. He and his militia
roared out of the Everglades on Easter Sunday – and
at last I had news of the movements of the world
– when power had been seized by a black junta
armed with missiles and rockets, and California
had seceded from the Union without so much as
a by-your-leave. Tossing fitfully in his bunk after
watching the TV news that night, the Colonel was
visited by a vision. The Son of Man, who looked,
to his unsurprise, very much like himself, dressed
in the uniform of the Green Berets, pointed West.

"I come," said the Colonel, "to bring, not peace,
but a sword."

His voice had hardly broken. It was the Children's
Crusade.

They asked me who I was and how I'd fallen in
with the pervert whom the officer had shot. I said,

my name was Eve and the man they so carelessly disposed of had been my husband. When I said that, I was overcome with the most desolating grief and burst out crying. Then the Colonel grew horribly embarrassed and sent his batman running off for a box of paper tissues and told me I should not cry, I must not: but he could give me no good reason why I ought not.

The little boys were abashed, at first, at the sight of a weeping woman and brought me bars of chocolate to console me but when I would not stop, they pelted me with stones to rid themselves of their embarrassment, and at last thrust me into the jeep again, to hide me, and off we drove, due West, leaving behind us a wake as straight as a die in the sand. While they drove, they sang holy songs in very sweet trebles and when I had cried away all my tears, I awoke a little from the deathly dream, that aghast, entranced lapse of consciousness, that parenthesis in the substance of the world, the trance of love.

I looked at the children with dulled eyes. They did not astonish me.

The Colonel wore a Mickey Mouse watch and cleaned his teeth three times a day, after every meal. He would not drink tea or coffee, only Coca-Cola. The house-keeper, the dedicated evangelist, was responsible for the indelible disfiguration of his tattoo – had led him by the hand to the parlour and fed him with candy while the needles buzzed. It had been perpetrated upon him before he had finished growing and the features of the disciples would subtly distort with the years, acquire the elongations of El Greco so his skin would soon mock the picture upon it, but he did not realise that and I thought, well, perhaps he will die before it spoils, since he is taking his little column right into the heart of the civil war.

The Colonel had a radio in his cabin on which to listen to the newscasts. It was tuned to a holy station in Salt Lake City which broadcast the New Testament continuously, twenty-four hours a day. When they came to the end of the Apocalypse, they started once again from the first book of Matthew. At particularly well-known passages, such as the Sermon on the Mount, all seventy-five little soldiers would join together and chant in unison; their pretty voices drowned the roar of the jeeps. They had the forlorn faces of orphans but their eyes were bright with hope.

The webbed wheels of the half-tracks dislocated the pale, shifting aridities below us until the rocks began to show their craggy teeth, and the flora – the spiked barrels and thin, barked fingers of cactus – indicated we had reached the edge of the void of negation, that centre-piece of sterility where the immortal remains of Tristessa de St Ange were lying.

The round horizon now cupped us in mountains; beyond the ridge, the Colonel told me, lay California and the Holy War against Blacks, Mexis, Reds, Militant Lesbians, Rampant Gays, etc etc etc. I thought he was a poor, motherless child who had never been suckled at a woman's breast, I felt sorry for him but did not care too much about his schemes, for was not Tristessa dead? Dead, and rotting, under the carrion sun.

We camped in the foothills of the mountains. They needed a good night's sleep before the descent into Southern California. They lit a bonfire to keep away the mountain lions and bivouacked around it in army surplus tents which they erected with the diligence and enthusiasm of boy scouts. The Colonel slept by himself. I was allocated a sleeping bag in the back of the jeep: there was nowhere else to house me. A guard kept watch at the fire.

From the fleecy inside of my sleeping bag, I watched the fat moon dispense indifferent lights upon the tumbled crags. When I remembered my memories, I could not sleep for grief. I'd never seen such a callous moon, no knife had ever caused such pain. The child on guard nodded at his post. Then I heard a rustling and scuffling beside me. I thought, here comes a mountain lion – and lay as still as Rousseau's gipsy; but, instead of a lion, it was the Colonel, poor child, who was frightened of so much darkness in his little tent and had come to me for comfort, had climbed into the sleeping bag with me and now buried his head in my breasts, where he sobbed out his fears as if he were much younger than fourteen and I was truly his mother. I stroked his bristling, cropped head and murmured what comfort I could, but his terrors were too great to be soothed by words and so he sobbed himself to sleep.

The guard lay stretched on the ground by the dying fire. It was long past moon-set. A perfect and impenetrable darkness surrounded the camp, a darkness with the texture of black sandpaper. I was free to run away, to run back to the grave in the sand, to lie down upon it and there to waste away from sorrow. I was very much struck by the emblematic beauty of this idea; to die for love! So much had I become the mortal, deathward-turning aspect of Tristessa.

With this, then, in mind, I climbed out of the sleeping-bag, taking care not to disturb the Colonel, picked up a sub-machine gun from his tent, and filled a canvas bag with tinned goods to eat on the journey from the food store in the quarter-master's half-track. Just as I picked up a can of corned beef, there was a gigantic explosion overhead.

The night sky opened in two dark halves and spilled out immense quantities of fire. I fell on my face. All the little soldiers woke up, screaming, and I could hear the Colonel wailing for me: "Eva! Eva!" They scrambled from their sleeping bags and grasped their weapons but there was nobody to fire at, for the sky now sealed itself over its wound and all was as it had been before. The poor boys milled about helplessly in the dark, tripping over one another and wailing. A gun went off by accident, BANG. They shrieked again and began to mumble prayers. I stayed where I had crawled under the jeep during this confusion until my dazzled eyes had recovered and I could make out their vague shapes. Then I ran rapidly through the disorder, humping my sack of provisions.

"Fire from heaven!" cried the Colonel; and then, again: "Eva! Where are you! Eva!" I clambered into the jeep, switched on the ignition and roared away; Eve was on the run again.

Eleven

Eve on the run again, under a sky fissured with artificial fire and the distant rumble of a bombardment –
a wild night; but I was pelting off towards my only
home, my lover's grave, and the signature of warfare
above me meant not so much to me as the memory
of a single one of Tristessa's kisses, I tell you, nothing
at all so much as the track of his footprint in the dust.
I jammed hard on the accelerator; soon sand foamed
about me. On, on! until, before me, approaching
me, I saw a constellation of little lights, a travelling
vee formation far away across the desert but bearing
down directly upon me at great speed. The rocket's
red glare lit up this technological cavalry in a flash of
synthetic lightning, which momentarily blanched a
grisly white the entire priestesshood of Cybele, silent
as a flock of birds, hundreds of them, the matriarchal
Valkyrie on newly souped-up sand-sleds, cutting off
all access to my darling. To go on would take me
straight into the arms of my Mother.

The explosions must have brought them out;
they, too, were coming with their guns, grenades
and missiles to join in the civil war in California. I

was caught in the cross-fire. I found myself far more afraid of Mother than mad to die where Tristessa lay; I made a jarring, screeching U-turn in a plume of upflung sand and then it was flat out the way I'd come – I pursued a course, now, that would lead me into the heart of the firework display, drove like a bat out of hell with the women's detachment, it seemed to me, hot on my heels. Perhaps they stopped to shoot it out with the Children's Crusade; but however it was, I'd lost them by the time I left the desert, the domain of the sun, the arena of metaphysics, the place where I became myself.

Towards dawn, I found myself, after my hectic flight, travelling along a pocked, cratered but still negotiable minor highway. Goodbye to the arid glamour of sterility! As it grew light, in the soft beginnings of a spring day, I found myself amid green, rolling country where groves of citrus were coming into odorous blossom, the lovely land where the lemon tree grows. I could see, tucked away in the low hills, stucco villas with pleasant gardens surrounding them, the turquoise flash of a swimming pool, the graceful exclamation point of cryptomeria. The road itself had taken the brunt of the air-raids around here; the telephone poles and power cables were all down, but, apart from that, everything seemed perfectly normal except there was not a soul to be seen. I might have been the only human left alive in all the world, Eve and Adam both, on a mission to repopulate this entire, devastated continent.

The fuel gauge stood at zero. I stopped for gas

at a self-service place where all seemed deserted;
too deserted, not even the whirr of cicadas, so
that, when I cut off the engine, a perfect silence
descended around me like a glass bell and trapped
me. I cautiously opened the door of the jeep and
a slug, of course, ripped through the windscreen,
missing me by inches. I had company. I flung
myself in the back of the vehicle and kept still.
A casement window flapped in the second storey
of the pink pasteboard and plywood building; a
pinkish rose had been trained up trellising on the
front, I remember, and there was a kid's pushbike
propped against a white-painted fence. The figure
of a man now appeared in the open window; he
had a broad, red, blank face, he carried a shotgun.
I kept so still he must have thought he'd killed me.
Then, to my astonishment, he burst out crying,
put the barrel of the shotgun in his mouth and
pulled the trigger. His headless trunk swayed for
a few moments before it toppled forward on to the
forecourt in front of me and that was that. The
silence resumed.

In the upstairs living room where he'd been
prowling at the window, I found two dead children
sprawled half on, half off an unmade sofa bed in
front of an extinguished television set, a boy of
about eleven, a girl of, say, thirteen, both still in
their pyjamas, both shot in the back. There was a
huge tank of tropical fish against one wall, but the
beautiful rose and gold carp now all floated belly
upwards on the surface of the scummed and stagnant
water. Only the flies in this room were alive. In the

kitchen on the ground floor, behind the workshop where jointed segments of automobiles lay where he'd left them, I found the corpse of a woman who had been shot in the stomach the previous day, judging by the condition of her rigor mortis and the depth of the busy shroud of flies that covered her. Her hair was still in rollers under a gauze scarf, she'd been gunned down with a lipstick in one hand and a mirror in the other. A viscid trickle of water drained out of the stinking refrigerator; no more power, evidently. A sparse breakfast had been set out in the dinette, just a packet of cornflakes, a can of dried milk, but they'd not had time to eat it. Among these pathetic remains, a newspaper – a single, ill-printed, smudged sheet, not a newspaper, a bulletin, that assured me freedom and democracy would triumph, the Free State of California held Los Angeles where it was putting down a few pockets of resistance. Missiles were pointing at San Francisco and the Bay Area, capital of the renegade Independent Republic of California. Civil war within the civil war. All householders, advised the bulletin, should barricade their property and mount armed guard twenty-four hours a day, conserve stocks of food and fuel, contact Free State aerial patrols by burning in their backyards or nearby vacant lots a cruciform shape in the grass. I did not like the sound of *that* at all. My welcome back to historicity! Only the flies stirring, in this slaughterhouse; chaos is come again. Who'd welcomed chaos, why – my former neighbour in New York, the Czech alchemist. How long since I'd thought of him? Welcome to anteriority,

Eve; now I know we are at the beginning of the beginning.

There was still gas in the pumps outside, so I filled my tank and drove on. But now I had a good deal more to think of than Tristessa. Ever since the interrupted continuum I refer to as myself had left Manhattan six – or was it seven or even eight months ago? – it had lived in systems which operated within a self-perpetuating reality; a series of enormous solipsisms, a tribute to the existential freedom of the land of free enterprise. But now I felt myself on the edge of a system of reality that might be perpetrated by factors entirely external to itself, and of a kind to prompt an honest red-neck pater-familias to butcher his entire family and leave his pets to starve. I switched on the radio in the jeep to see if I could find news, any news at all. But, though I twisted the dial in all directions, I only flushed out a random crackling from the airwaves, a silence more ominous than any newscast or even than those continuous transmissions of military music that always accompany coups. Even the gospel station in Salt Lake City had disappeared from the airwaves. And still I saw nobody on the highway, though the next filling station I passed had been the scene of a battle; the building was gutted and blackened as if it had been shelled, a burned-out station wagon lay on its back like a dead roach in front of the pumps. Once a plane, a small Cessna, appeared briefly on the edge of the horizon. Otherwise, I was alone among the blossoming citrus, heading, I assumed, in the general direction of Los Angeles.

I did not know for certain. I knew nothing of the geography of California and there was no map in the jeep.

But I continued on for I was filled with a raging curiosity to see the end of the world.

The glossy foliage of lemon, orange and eucalyptus glittered in the morning sun as if their leaves were made of beaten tin, and there were palms, too, with calloused trunks and stiff, creaking topknots, lines of palms along this avenue so eerily denuded of traffic; but, for all the tropic vegetation that surrounded me, there was no sense of a lavish over-spill of nature. The stony soil under the crude, primitive shapes of the palms looked as if snakes would like best to breed there, a dry stoniness that bred only the harshest, least succulent verdure. Now, fast, sudden, unexpected, a mountain range loomed to my left, with cruel, purplish outlines; all around me gave me the sense of trompe l'oeil, of theatre, of a stage set for some ghastly catastrophe and I myself as yet the only actor who'd appeared. And still nothing moved, not those glossy leaves, heavy, still, carved from glass, nor the blossoms slick as immortelles. Sometimes a screen door banged on the porch of a bungalow. Once I saw a dog in front of the boarded-up reception cabin of a motel called the Forty Winks Motel but it lay with its head on its paws, rapt, immobile, and did not look up as I passed. I drove through little towns, the drug-stores looted, the cables down, a sense of barricades; then the groves and the vertical stripes of the vineyards, again. The road before me was straight as a die.

Then I came to one of those all-purpose pleasure domes, entertainment area and shopping centre and parking lot all at once, stranded out here in the middle of the fields in the way they are, set back from the highway like a concrete citadel which at night should flash with neon; there was a huge arch that led to a commercial plaza, a giant parking lot and a Spanish-style bowling alley-cum-bar-cum-restaurant with a giant bowling pin before it, at the roadside. As soon as I set eyes on the rough-cast off-white plaster and ginger tile of this place, everything exploded. The front wall came away entirely, like the detachable front of a doll's house, in a rushing roar of gelignite, and all began to flame merrily. Flushed from the building, half a dozen fleeing figures – first sign of life that morning: and each one fell, picked off by snipers lodged in the blazing ruins.

Simultaneously, a mine blew up the stretch of road directly in front of me.

Action stations! I ran the jeep into the side of the road, left the engine running, abandoned ship. Bullets zipped round me as I made for the shopping plaza, where I judged there would be more cover, but as soon as I got under the Hispanic arch, I heard the rattle of gunfire here too; I ducked through the shattered window of a supermarket, felt the breeze of a bullet pass my cheek, heard it plug the wall, dropped to my face in the broken glass, crawled towards a gondola still laden with fancy goods – paper napkins, cardboard cups, doilies – crouched behind it, shivering. The supermarket had clearly been looted several times. Flour was trampled into the floor, sugar crunched underfoot, spilled jams and syrups, reek of spoiled dairy food, a black scum of flies swimming in the broken refrigerator cabinets. The participants in a hand-to-hand struggle appeared and disappeared in the riven surfaces of the square, leaping, falling, screaming amid white clouds of dust from descending masonry. Bullets whined. Running feet. I could not make head or tail out of what was going on.

A man in green, brown-blotched army fatigues dropped briefly through the supermarket window and crouched to reload a hand-gun, but before he could fire it, the stuttering hail of a machine-gun caught him and spun him round and let him drop. When they brought the machine-gun into action, the incident was almost over. A handful of bloody survivors beat a rough and ready retreat through the Hispanic arch, firing from their hips as they ran. The last man out tossed a hand grenade behind, up and up went the arch in a heavy rain of debris, and up, too, went the facade of the supermarket. I was drowned in falling plaster, a brick-bat struck my head, everything vanished.

I came to myself to find a snout of cold metal poking me not ungently in the ribs and, when I opened my eyes, I saw a youth with black curls, a single earring in his left ear, dungarees, workshirt, kneeling over me. I lay on my back in a mound of rubble, my head pounding, bleeding from a dozen tiny cuts but no bones were broken, no serious damage was done. The boy who'd nudged me awake with his rifle now spoke to me in a

language I could not understand, though I realised
it was Spanish. After a moment, when he saw I
could not understand a word he was saying, he laid
down his rifle, put his arms around me and helped
me to my feet. I was too dizzy to walk alone and
he folded me against his shoulder to half-carry me
across the upheaval of the plaza to the cave-like
remains of a sporting goods shop where, amid heaps
of splintered surf-boards, some members of a group
of uniformless soldiery were engaged in fortifying a
machine-gun nest on the roof with sandbags while
others were lining up a column of grim-faced prisoners, and still others tended their own wounds or
those of others. I suppose there were about thirty or
thirty-five of them, some black, some brown, some
yellow, some white, most young, some very young,
without a flag or any insignia, a raggle-taggle bunch
of well-armed hobos.

A boy of about seventeen with blood-caked hair
and a face contorted by pain lay on his back on what
had been the counter of the shop; his right leg had
been blasted off below the knee and a black girl in
shorts and singlet and gun-belt, all besmeared and
beblubbered with filth, was giving him an injection,
an operation she performed with great care and skill,
even with love. Scraps of plaster had caught in her
wiry hair; they reminded me of how Leilah, my last
duchess, had stuck beads and little diamanté birds
and artificial flowers in the shrubbery of her Afro.
A couple of young girls with old faces set up a
stretcher for the wounded one, a craggy old man
assembled dressings. As soon as the boy sank down

through a sea of babblings into unconsciousness, the
black girl turned to look at this new prisoner.

Her eyes were veiled with weariness but, all the
same, their shapes reminded me of the shapes of
Leilah's vanished eyes; how long since I'd thought
of Leilah? But this girl wore a scarlet armband
bound round the upper part of her arm with a
female circle printed on it and, within the circle,
a truncated column. Oh, god. My heart began to
pound fearfully. Her almost familiar regard rested
on me for a long, interrogatory moment; then she
smiled, with a tentative, ironic welcome.

"Eve?" queried the black girl, hesitating a little as
though she did not want to offend me by a mistake.
"Evelyn?"

And, still tentative yet beautifully – what? for-
giving? conciliatory? magnanimous? – she held out
her battle-stained hands to me.

Why did you never tell me who your mother
was, Leilah?

How could I have told you so that you would have
believed me? I never said she was a scrubwoman,
you took that for granted, a gross assumption. I
told you she lived on the West Coast. Would you
have believed me if I'd told you?

Her laughter. The same as it had been at first, that
unmuddled spring of freshness in it. She laughed
at me quite kindly and told me they'd wiped
out a nasty little pocket of resistance here in the
Benito Cereno shopping centre and Relaxarama,
had scored a handy cache of arms, the severely
wounded would now be shipped off to the field

hospital at HQ and I could go off with them; or would I stay here, where they were going to fortify the shopping centre and man a road-block to cope with the streams of refugees who would soon be on the move? No, the Free State did *not* hold Los Angeles, that was lying propaganda; a dozen factions were warring over the remains of Southern California and though the rightist group calling itself the Free State had overthrown the black junta who'd first taken California out of the Union, three of its leaders had been assassinated in an armed ambush while our comrades in the North launched the air bombardment last night, though Northern California was in as much confusion as the South and – and seeing my bewilderment, she paused, shrugged, said: "It's been a long time coming, but it's come."

The immensity of the catastrophe and her bland and irreproachable composure in the face of it overwhelmed me. And her presence here, her wholly unexpected and yet perfectly fitting presence at the end and the beginning of the world – further, her absolute disinterest in my changed state! Her straightforward and unequivocal acceptance of my female condition! Nothing in her manner, which was conspicuously gentle, nor in her dress, which was ragged, indicated she was their leader; only the spontaneous if undisciplined respect of the other ranks proved it.

When I said I'd stay, they found me a pair of old sneakers to put on my bare feet and set me to washing the wounded. When the wounded had been taken away in a haphazard fleet of station wagons, delivery trucks, ice-cream vans, I pitched in with the preparation of a meal from stores retrieved from the supermarket. We fixed a bonfire in the middle of the Plaza and slung above it an iron cauldron they'd found in the storeroom of a boutique, it must have been used for a Hallowe'en window display. Somebody discovered a can of red paint in a wrecked hardware store and effortfully lettered on a remaining wall the legend, YEAR ONE: Leilah was now occupied with a radio transmitter, chattering away in morse. I caught sight of her watching me abstractedly as she tapped away at the keys of her machine; I saw no surprise nor satisfaction in her eyes at all, only a detached, impersonal kindness. Leilah but no longer Leilah; what's become of the hour of Manhattan? Had she all the time been engaged on guerrilla warfare for her mother? Had that gorgeous piece of flesh and acquiescence been all the time a show, an imitation, an illusion? Her hair still sprang out in a contention of small curls and her skin looked, still, like refreshed velvet, but the deadly passivity of the naked dancer had been washed off with the paint. And had she really suffered when I'd fathered a child on her, was it real blood that spilled on the floor of the taxi when she came back to me, torn, mutilated, from the Haitian abortionist? And was my body her revenge? A dull, almost lulling pain throbbed in my temples; she smiled at me, a cool, bland, impersonal smile.

Towards the middle of the afternoon, after they'd shot the prisoners and I'd helped bury them, as

we ate our chilli con carne, she came and sat
beside me.

"History overtook myth," she said. "And rendered it obsolete. Mother tried to take history into
her own hands but it was too slippery for her to hold.
Time has a way of running away with itself, though
she set all the symbols to work; she constructed a
perfect archetype."

And she gently, almost sorrowfully, touched my
breasts. She asked me what had become of me since
I ran away from Beulah and set all her mother's
plans awry; I told her of my bondage to Zero and
the desecration of Tristessa's house. When I spoke
his name, my sadness overcame me, my eyes filled
with tears.

"His name has all the poignancy of hopelessness
in its whispering sibilants," said Leilah softly, as to
herself. "Abandoned on this great continent like a
star in space, an atomised, fragmented existence, his
cock stuck in his asshole so that he himself formed
the uroborus, the perfect circle, the vicious circle,
the dead end."

"I thought it had been the best kept secret in the
world."

"Years ago, long before I was born, he went
to my mother when she was working in LA as a
cosmetic surgeon, all very hush-hush, like a state
secret. You can guess what it was he wanted. She
told me he offered her a million dollars, a million
dollars to match his function to his form, the poor,
bewildered thing."

"Why wouldn't she do it?"

"Mama told me, he was too much of a woman, already, for the good of the sex; and, besides, when she subjected him to the first tests, she was struck by what seemed to her the awfully ineradicable quality of his maleness."

The flames of our camp fires began to die down. The Chicano who'd found me among the rubble had got hold of a guitar and was singing quietly in his native language, in a fine, rich baritone.

"Historicity rendered myth unnecessary," said Leilah. "The Priestesses of Cybele have left off simulating miraculous births for a while and have turned into storm-troopers. As for me, as you know, I used to rouge my nipples and dance a dance called the End of the World, to lead the unwary into temptation – "

Just then a field telephone rang and she spoke into it for a long time. I could not hear what she said, though I guessed the discussion concerned me because she glanced at me from time to time and once smiled at me, as if reassuringly. When she hung up, she suggested to the battalion it was time to bivouac and tugged me to my feet from where I'd been huddled by the fire. "I've got to take you on a trip, Eve." We would leave the ruins in her armoured car, with a flask of coffee and a pack of sandwiches to sustain us; urgent mission to the coast, she told her brigade, personal reasons – I'm going to see my mother.

When she said that, the hairs on my nape helplessly rose, though now I had the protection of the goddess's natural daughter. But the glint of steel in

Leilah's eyes brought me to heel and I obediently climbed into the vehicle beside her.

"Don't be afraid," she said; "Mother has voluntarily resigned from the god-head, for the time being. When she found she could not make time stand still, she suffered a kind of . . . nervous breakdown. She has become quite gentle and introspective. She has retired to a cave by the sea for the duration of the hostilities."

Should we do that with all the symbols, Leilah? Put them away, for a while, until the times have created a fresh iconography?

Shall we do that, Leilah?

"Lilith is my name," she said. "I called myself Leilah in the city in order to conceal the nature of my symbolism. If the temptress displays her nature, the seducee is put on his guard. Lilith, if you remember, was Adam's first wife, on whom he begot the entire race of the djini. All my wounds will magically heal. Rape only refreshes my virginity. I am ageless, I will outlive the rocks."

She laughed self-deprecatingly. We were driving along a mountain road; across the mountains lay the ocean.

"'And what is the function of such a being?'" she asked in her fresh, dark voice. "'To interpret and convey messages to the gods from men and to men from the gods, prayers and sacrifices from the one and commands and rewards from the other.' That's how Plato, for one, defined us."

There was a familiar crispness in her vowels; I detected in them, somewhere, the cut-glass vowels of an East Coast university and this clue led me directly to Sophia, blonde, stern, monomamiliar Sophia, my governess under the earth, as if I now met one girl who had previously been dual – Lilith, all flesh, Sophia, all mind.

"And when there was a consensus agreement on the nature of the symbolic manifestations of the spirit, no doubt Divine Virgins, Sacred Harlots and Virgin Mothers served a useful function; but the gods are all dead, there's a good deal of redundancy in the spirit world."

But *you've* found yourself a new job, Leilah!

"I'm afraid we'll have more difficulty in finding satisfactory employment for you, though, Eve."

Towards the north, the sky never grew completely dark but remained stained with a smoky rose; when I drew Lilith's attention to it, she stated without emotion:

"Those are the flames of Los Angeles."

Leilah, Lilith: now I see you are your mother's daughter, that immobility, that vast and sentient repose – what's become of the slut of Harlem, my girl of bile and ebony! She can never have objectively existed, all the time mostly the projection of the lusts and greed and self-loathing of a young man called Evelyn, who does not exist, either. This lucid stranger, Lilith, also known as Leilah, also, I suspect, sometimes masquerading as Sophia or the Divine Virgin, seems to offer me disinterested friendship, though in the past I might have caused her pain; I have no option but to accept it. I am quite alone in California. I am a stranger here. I am a British citizen. I do not understand the political situation. There is a war on. And my heart is broken, my heart is broken.

The same moon that took Tristessa and me into its polarised embrace in the desert now swung up into the sky. After a while, I drifted off to sleep, my head wedged against the steel door, a very deep, dreamless sleep as if Lilith's presence were some protection against the perils of the night; when I woke in the brownish, discoloured dawn, the first thing I saw was the limitless expanse of the Pacific lying before and below me, ridged and grey as a slate roof, vast, quiescent. Landlocked so long, I'd forgotten the omniverous inscrutability of the sea, how it nibbles the earth with a mouth of water, how it ignores us.

We jounced along an ill-kept coast road. A tide full of broken beams, cars floating with their wheels in the air, spars and coffee tables, television sets, refrigerators, loudspeakers, turntables, hulks of little pleasure boats smashed against the rocks, cast carapaces of mobile homes – the ignoble detritus of the civilisation of half a state tumbled into the water from bombed-out waterside developments further up the coast lapped and knocked at the breakwater. I remember particularly a monstrous dog's head, in brown plaster, head of a dachshund in a bow tie and a chef's cap – it had rotated on a pole, I recalled from my spell on the road, outside a chain of hot-dog stands, the eponymous sign-board of the Doggie Diners, now consigned to the enormous refuse bin of the ocean.

"Oh, yes," said Lilith, "a terrible devastation." She smiled with a secret pleasure. "The cities of California are burning like the Cities of the Plain."

And she herself had danced the dance called the End of the World to invoke retribution upon Gomorrah; but now she was changed, she was part of the purging.

Here, only seabirds swooped over great cliffs and there was no sign of life until the road brought us to a broadish bay with a wide beach of pebbles, and then petered out into the track it had threatened to become for the last few miles we had been upon it. On this beach, a lone, mad old lady sat in a wicker garden chair that had once been painted bright pink. A sack containing tinned food lay on the ground beside her. To her left stood a rustic, folding, garden table bearing a plate, a knife and fork, a can opener and a bottle of vodka. We heard her voice as soon as Lilith switched off the ignition; she was singing popular songs of the thirties in a thin voice of cracked yet piercing sweetness. She did not turn her head to look at us, perhaps she didn't hear us.

It was an impressive head. The hair was dyed a brave canary yellow and piled in an elaboration of many tiers of curls, giving the general impression of a very expensive ice-cream sundae. All was decorated with peek-a-boo bows of pale pink silk ribbon and would have looked well under a glass dome on grandmother's mantelpiece. She was wearing a two-piece bathing costume in a red and white spotted fabric and, round her shoulders, a stole of

glossy and extravagant blonde fur but her flesh was
wrinkled and ravaged and sagged from her bones.
Her face was very dirty but magnificently painted;
a fresh coating of white powder and scarlet lipstick
and maroon rouge must have been added that very
morning. She was quite oblivious of our presence.
She sat on her chair and sang of the lights of
Broadway, of foggy days in London Town and
how she'd learned her lesson but she wished she
were in love again. Her swimming eyes had retreated
deeply into her head down cavernous sockets frosted
with glittering turquoise eye-grease. Her fingernails
were fully six inches long and lacquered a glinting
red, though badly chipped and scratched. She wore
high-heeled silver sandals on her gnarled old feet and
sat facing the ocean like the guardian of the shore; her
fissured high soprano mingled with the slumbrous
chords of the sea. Leilah watched her with a faint
smile of pity, or irony.

When this old lady came to the end of "Everything
is peaches down in Georgia", she rose to her feet,
walked stiffly to a gaunt bush in the lee of the
cliff, turned her back modestly to the seagulls,
pulled down the lower half of her bathing costume,
evacuated her bowels, scooped up a handful of earth,
scattered it over the mess, performed one or two
physical jerks that made her dangling flesh judder
and then returned to her table, where she now dug
busily in her sack. When she found a can of beans,
she opened it, scraped the contents on to her plate
and decorously ate them with the aid of her knife
and fork, set the knife and fork together again with

a clang, then reached for her bottle and emptied three inches of vodka down her throat. Her Adam's apple, prominent as that of an old man, registered each gulp with a vigorous convulsion. After she'd put the bottle down again, she gave a loud, satisfied belch and once again broke into song.

Half-hidden behind the bush where she performed her natural functions was a little boat drawn up far out of reach of the tide, a neat little rowing boat, with oars, all complete, made out of a cheerful mauve plastic. How had it got here? Had she herself rowed it all the way here with a cargo of table and chair, food and drink, rouge and powder, from the burned-out shell of a haven for senior citizens in Malibu? Or had she salvaged it from a backyard or a parking lot on her foot-sore way to the sea, it was just the kind of boat you strap to the top of a car and take to the beach on a Saturday afternoon, for a few hours pleasure.

She continued to sing. Only her lips moved fractionally in her immobile face, stiffened as it was by the mask of cosmetics and grime. Her repertoire was endless, as soon as she finished one song she began at once on another like a mechanical contrivance. Lilith let in the clutch and we rolled slowly past, behind her, but this sprightly refugee never looked round even once.

Lilith wanted to know if I thought she should take the old lady back with her to a refugee camp and settle her in or did I think she was best off here, at least until her vodka ran out, and Lilith would see to it she was brought more when that happened . . . how would

the old ones fare, in the post-apocalyptic world?
Might she not be better off in her dream, as long
as it lasted? I did not answer her; I was preoccupied
in watching the complicated aerodynamics of the
great, white sea-birds who glided on the turbulent
currents of the upper air above the shifting ocean.
Lilith took my silence for assent.

"Then I shall leave her," decided Lilith. "Maybe
rig up a shelter for her, in case there's a shower."

We rounded the promontory into a little, secret
cove, jolting over the uneven ground, and she
parked. Coffee and sandwiches; breakfast. I felt
a rising objection to the displays of conspicuous
humanity she insisted on making. I knew her secret.
I knew she could not abdicate from her mythology
as easily as that; she still had a dance to dance, even
if it was a new one, even if she performed it with
absolute spontaneity.

When our small breakfast was done, she took me
out of the car and led me a little way along the
shore. The pebbles bruised my feet through the
worn-out soles of my sneakers. The sea remained
calm, there was scarcely the frill of a wave to be
seen; the day remained sullen. She led me to a fissure
in the rock-face so narrow a full-grown adult could
only crawl through it sideways. From this fissure
gushed a little fountain of fresh water that moistened
the shingle into which it disappeared. Leilah handed
me a stout flashlight. Then I realised I must slide
into the living rock all alone to rendezvous with my
maker.

Lilith gave me a little kiss on the cheek, patted

my rump, told me to quit stalling, to get on with it while she went back to see if there was anything she could do for the mad old lady.

I saw there was nothing for it but I must fold myself into the interstice of rock so in I went and my sneakers were thoroughly soaked in a moment by the freezing little stream, my skin scored and grazed by the cruel embrace of the rock that kneaded my tender nipples unmercifully and bruised and jarred my knees and elbows. My hair snared on little outcroppings; the flashlight illuminated nothing before me except the inexpressive faces of rock. Nevertheless, I edged my way forward, flat as a flounder. Every movement necessitated the most extreme exertion; I was soon drenched with sweat. The passage was choked, airless, dank, and a faint reek of rotten eggs hovered above the sulphurated streamlet. The crack of light behind me and the cerulean glimpse of the sea gradually diminished; I was making progress, pressed as I was like a cheese, oozing forward. Then the day vanished altogether and I was committed to the rocks, poking before me with that little spoke of light.

All at once, a lowering of the spirits.

My return to the world only confirms my permanent exile.

I continued to edge my way crabwise along the crevice. Mother has inserted herself in the most hermetic of fall-out shelters. She clearly plotted to survive the holocaust.

Meanwhile, above my head, the state of California progresses through a series of transformations. But

Eve negotiates with the concrete regression of this cave. Eve returns to her mother.

But however hard I push against the rock, I seem to get no closer to Mother, though the little stream through which I wade is now up to my knees and grows warmer, a soft and generous warmth. Then, probing too vigorously before me with my flashlight, it knocks against an unexpected jag of rock; startled, I drop it – whoosh! like a descending rocket, into the little stream, where my only light is instantly doused.

Darkness and silence.

The rocks between which I am pressed as between pages of a gigantic book seem to me to be composed of silence; I am pressed between the leaves of a book of silence. This book has been emphatically closed.

I am an inconvenient relic of the Cities of the Plain. I'll petrify here, like Lot's wife!

Familiar panic of the entry into earth's entrails.

Spreadeagled across the rock face, I made one last lunge forward. My groping right hand encountered empty air. I lost balance and toppled forward into a wide, shallow pool of pleasantly warm water. I sat up in the water, taking great gulps of the fresh, pure air that now blew from an invisible source into my face. As I did so, there was a mechanical click and the light came on, a naked bulb dangling from the high ceiling of a large cave.

But the cave was quite empty, although, hung over the back of a chair standing beside the pool on a floor of clean, dry, packed sand, was a clean towel.

The chair was straight-backed and rush-seated, in the style of the godly and austere Shakers. So she's brought her furniture with her, has she?

When I'd soaked in the pool long enough and taken the opportunity to rinse out my hair, which was full of sand and dust, I climbed out and rubbed myself down, kicked off my sodden tennis shoes and hung my overalls over the back of the chair to dry. There was a mirror propped against the rugged wall, a fine mirror in a curly, gilt frame; but the glass was broken, cracked right across many times so it reflected nothing, was a bewilderment of splinters and I could not see myself nor any portion of myself in it. The water bubbled into the pool from a rather larger fissure in the rock than the one from which I'd just emerged and I judged that through it I must crawl and that I must go naked, that this was part of my ordeal.

This corridor was wider but lower. I must crawl against the gentle current of the stream and now I'm in danger of drowning if I don't hold my head up high, or if I hold it too high in the dark and bump against an invisible projection so that I'm, however momentarily, stunned, and drop down with my face under the surface, mouth and nostrils filled at once with water. What an assault course! Death by pressing, death by drowning. And I know by that almost palpable sense of mystery Mother exudes as helplessly as a bitch on heat that she's waiting for me at the end of this system of caves, the gross godhead of an arcane theology that has gone underground, now, as the witches did in the early Middle Ages.

I emerged in a smaller cave, a cave almost filled by water that was now at blood heat, emitting a faint steam and a scarcely tolerable stench of sulphur. And this cave was filled with a familiar, dim, red light for which I could perceive no source. There was a ledge of rock above the water which now lapped round my breasts; I grasped the edge of this ledge, which cut and bruised my fingers badly, and with a good deal of effort and a painful buffeting from the inhospitable granite, I pulled myself up on it. No towel laid out for me, this time, but a white linen cloth spread as for a picnic and laid out upon it, a photograph, a glass flask and a mystery object wrapped up in a scrap of paper.

The photograph, of course, was a glossy publicity still of Tristessa at the height of her beauty, with her hair coiled in loop upon serpentine loop on her head, in her ears little hearts, an evening gown of black satin with gardenias against her dazzling throat: ah, how glorious it is to be a woman! And she has signed herself across the right hand corner, in a strange, spiky hand: "Loving you always, Tristessa de St A." I choked on a sob and a fury gripped me; I seized the photograph and ripped it in four pieces, across, across and let the fragments drop into the bubbling pool below me, where they floated on the surface like little boats, or white feathers, until the busy current sucked them away, down through the fissure, into the lower cave. To my surprise, I saw a red stain, blood, appear on the cloth where the photograph had been.

Next to this bloodstain was the glass flask, which

was of a strange, swan-necked shape. I had seen such a flask in the laboratory of Baroslav, the Czech alchemist. The flask contained a large chunk of amber, about a pound in weight, like a section of smoky honeycomb, a clouded yellow in colour. Trapped in this amber was the feather of a bird. I guessed some action was expected of me so I picked up the flask and warmed it between my hands. Soon the amber began to melt – no, not precisely to melt; as I chafed the flask as if it were a brandy snifter, the amber began, very slowly, to soften, or, rather, to become viscous.

As I watched this process, it came to me that the word "duration" was utterly meaningless.

As I continued to watch the process, it came to me that the word "progression" was just as meaningless as the word "duration."

Then I felt that sick sudden sensation of falling that means one's heart has missed a beat. I realised I had no sensation at all of the passage of time.

Now a sweet, clean scent of pine drifted through the cave; at first I thought it blew in from the open air, some complicated system of internal passages and black draughts. But no. It rose up like incense from the glass flask in my hands, from the amber that was becoming the heavy dew of resin cast by the amber forests of a remote past that was, as I turned the flask round and round in my warm palms, becoming, with an infinite slowness, the present of this red cave.

The amber was undergoing a process of reversal in which I and the rock itself were involved; the rock refreshed. The waters rushed and gurgled more exuberantly, and then more exuberantly still. I peered around me and saw rude shapes of bison and huge-helmed stag scrawled on the walls in faded pigments which, as I looked, grew brighter, their outlines firmer.

Time is running back on itself.

The amber in the flask had now reached the consistency of tar and the glass was too hot for me to hold any more. I put it back on the cloth. I unwrapped the little parcel beside it; at first I did not recognise the object it contained, a little bar of yellow metal hanging from a chain, a pendant. Then I saw it was the ingot of alchemical gold I'd given Leilah in the darkness and confusion of the city, and now, in this roundabout way, her mother gave it back to me, pierced on a chain so that I could wear it round my neck like a locket. I thought I might need something with which to pay the fatal ferryman, so I slipped my new necklace over my head, and the half-inch of gold fitted snugly into the hollow of my throat.

And that was the second cave.

The aperture through which I must now go was large and wide enough for me to walk through, like a human being, not creep like a spider or splash like an amphibian. I stepped over the white cloth towards it and, as I did so, I knocked over the aludel; the liquid resin spread, very, very slowly over the white cloth like spilled syrup. The smell of pines in the cave was now overpowering, and followed me through this final passage, and increased in intensity the further I went.

This new passage was, at first, quite dry but as I progressed, it grew warmer and warmer; the walls dripped with a moisture more viscid, more clinging than water, and the dim, red glow of the second cavern receded behind me but its colour did not leave me. My hand stretched before me was drenched, now, with a bloody dew.

The rock had softened or changed its substance; the textures under my enquiring fingers were soft and yielding. Time no longer passed. Now the dew felt like slime; this slime coated me. The walls of this passage shuddered and sighed at first almost imperceptibly, so that I mistook it for my own breathing. But their pulsations exert greater and greater pressure on me, draw me inward.

Walls of meat and slimy velvet.

Inward.

A visceral yet perfectly rhythmic agitation ripples the walls, which ingest me.

I'm not so scared as once I would have been, to go worming my way through the warm meat of the insides of the earth, for I know, now, that Mother is a figure of speech and has retired to a cave beyond consciousness. Everything takes place more slowly than you can believe possible. I have been subdued to the leisurely pace of Eocene time. The flask with the liquefying amber in it is a time-piece that tells me that above me blow the pines that grow where the sea will one day cover them, when the sun cools a little. In these woods grow beech, chestnut, maple, holly, mistletoe, juniper, olive, sandalwood, laurel, geranium, camelia . . . the ants and spiders and little scorpions will not change their shapes much, although the sea-lilies that will petrify long before I'm born now unfurl and blossom on the banks of the ocean. At that time, there was a bird called "archaeopteryx" whose fossil will be found in the schist of Solenhofen; bird and lizard both at once. a being composed of the contradictory elements of air and earth. From its angelic aspect spring the whole family tree of feathered, flying things and from its reptilian or satanic side the saurians, creepy crawlers, crocs, the scaled leaper and the lovely little salamander. The archaeopteryx has feathers on its back but bones in its tail, as well; claws on the tips of its wings; and a fine set of teeth. One of those miraculous, seminal, intermediate beings brushed against a pendant tear of rosin in the odorous and primeval amber forests and left behind a feather.

A miraculous, seminal, intermediate being whose nature I grasped in the desert.

The birds of the air shed all their feathers, which softly fall to the ground; scales now appear on their little bodies.

I am inching my way towards the beginning and the end of time.

It started in small ways. Perfumes broke from bottles which instantly resolved to sand as the dressing tables on which they'd stood flung roots down into the soil and sprouted leaves; back into the jasmine and the tuberose leapt the volatile oils, congealed again to ambergris inside the great, floating, gentle whale, into the genitals of the musk-rat and the musk-deer.

Rivers neatly roll up on themselves like spools of film and turn in on to their own sources. The final drops of the Mississippi, the Ohio, the Hudson, tremble on a blade of grass; the sun dries them up, the grass sinks back into the earth.

The foal leaps back into its mother's womb; the gravid mare sniffs the air, which smells of entropy, and takes fright, trots briskly back down the sinuous by-ways of evolution, a labyrinth like Ariadne's, past caves filled with sleeping bats who do not change their shapes as she goes by, through successive generations of her own ancestors; her hoof shrinks, now it's only the middle fingernail of the five toes of her paws. What stumpy little legs she has. She scampers away into the Tertiary forests, her bulging belly shrinks, she will produce no offspring as tribute to evolution. She herself becomes smaller and smaller until, in the alchemical vase, she becomes a solution of amino-acids and a tuft of hair, and then dissolves into the amniotic sea.

A brackish and marine smell now fills my nostrils, the odour of the sea within me.

But I myself will soon produce a tribute to evolution.

The walls of meat expelled me. Without a cry, I fell into a darkness like the antithesis of light, an immensity of darkness, the final cave through which now marched, animating the darkness, the parade of the great apes, which wound me back on the spool of time that now wound up. My shaggy breast, my great, carved brow with the germ of a brain behind it. I have forgotten how I picked up a stone and shattered a nut with it. The sound of the sea becomes omnipresent, the sea, which washes away all memory and retains it.

I have come home.

The destination of all journeys is their beginning.

I have not come home.

I emitted, at last, a single, frail, inconsolable cry like that of a new-born child. But there was no answering sound at all in that vast, sonorous place where I found myself but the resonance of the sea and the small echo of my voice. I called for my mother but she did not answer me.

"Mama – mama – -mama!"

She never answered.

Speleological apotheosis of Tiresias – Mother, having borne her, now abandons her daughter forever.

The wide mouth of this cave opened on to the rocky foreshore, where I could see Lilith sitting by the water's edge, with a ruck-sack she'd brought from the armoured car beside her; this strange day was almost over, the setting sun stroked with lateral fingers of light the waves across which she was skimming pebbles. The motion of her arm allowed me to observe she'd lost a breast, it must have been recently. She smiled at me and raised her eyebrows in a question to which I could not reply; I sat down beside her and let the wavelets splash my bare feet. She took a chocolate bar from her bag and shared it with me. I made a little boat out of the silver paper and set it to sail for China.

"What if Tristessa made you pregnant?" she

said. "Your baby will have two fathers and two mothers."

The waves washed my little craft back to my feet. I relaunched it. Preoccupied with my game, I nodded vaguely. Leilah now dived into her ruck-sack and produced a long, metal box about the size of an old-fashioned glove box. It was enamelled white. She nudged me to secure my wandering attention, for now my little boat was successfully bobbing towards the rouged tracks of the sunset, and snapped this box open. It was a miniature portable refrigerator. Inside, on a bed of dry ice, lay the set of genitals which had once belonged to Evelyn.

"You can have them back, if you still want them."

I burst out laughing and shook my head. She closed the box and sent it skimming over the waves, as she had done her pebbles; it skidded a longish way across the water until the crest of a breaker rose up and swallowed it. Then Lilith and I sat and watched the ocean suck at the beach for a while; the tide from Asia was once more coming in. She asked me, did I want to come back to camp with her; but she must warn me, that life would be hard for a pregnant woman during the civil war, the fight would be a long one. If I preferred to stay here quietly until my time came, she'd bring me a camping stove, bedding, stores and a few weapons to protect myself – and I could keep an eye on the mad old lady, too. Lilith, then, took it for granted that I was pregnant; and under her solicitous chatter, the surface of her speech, there was a ground-swell

Angela Carter

of necessity, I knew I had no option but to remain here. She gave me my exile, since I did not want my old self back; as soon as I realised this, I began to wonder if I might not in some way escape.

Lilith gave me a sleeping bag and some blankets from the armoured car, a pack of iron rations and a can to collect water in. She said she'd be back next day with more equipment or, if she couldn't make it personally, she'd send a couple of the others. She guessed the Free Staters wouldn't bother me, out here in the wilds on the coast, but she gave me a pistol and ammunition, just in case. Then I knew she was going to desert me and I'd a wild impulse to shoot her with this pistol but I suppressed it; I don't know where it came from, except humiliation at being an object of charity, of pity, for I knew in my heart, that, in her heart, Lilith pitied me just because of the exile to which she believed I was condemned. I walked with her to the armoured car, all the same, and there she abruptly kissed me and hugged me before she drove away. Long after she'd disappeared round the promontory, I heard the engine diminishing into the night.

That was the last I saw of Lilith.

A great explosion in the north shed petals of white light over everything and then the night closed over on itself like flesh on a wound. I wrapped one of the store of blankets around myself and contemplated getting myself a small meal of something or other but I couldn't face eating, and I didn't want to sleep in that damned, draughty, echoing cave, either. I decided to visit my companion, although a light drizzle had begun to fall, a sad, ominous, almost rain flavoured with ashes which greased the rocks of the foreshore so that I slipped and stumbled across them.

I heard her before I saw her; she still sat in her wicker chair and sang out bravely. I can't think when she slept. Perhaps she never slept. I saw that, in order to protect her from the elements, Lilith had opened a large, pink, paper parasol and planted it in the shingle behind her; this parasol was the twin of the one Sophia had unfurled in the desert when I was captured. Another explosion, nearer at hand, a huge one! A little hail of spent cinders pattered on her beach umbrella but the old lady never interrupted her song. When I saw her skiff pulled up by the tree, a plan came to me; but when I picked up the skiff – I could carry it easily in my arms – she stopped singing at once; she turned her head and I saw her misted eyes wander about the foreshore. There was only a brownish star-light but the sulphurous incandescence of the sky made it possible for me to see quite clearly.

"What have we here?" she said.

"Eve," I said as tenderly as I could, as if I were a friendly visitor she'd known since my childhood. "Only Eve."

She nodded her grave, stately head as if she recognised me at once.

"Why are you taking my boat away, Eve? When my last can was eaten, I was going to defecate for the last time under my tree, to say goodbye to the world in the most typically human fashion and then

I'd planned to climb into my little boat and sail away. It's not a boat, it's a coffin."

"Yes," I said. "I understand." But I did not put the skiff down. "I'm sorry I must steal your coffin."

Her eyes moved all the time but never focused on me, so I realised she was blind.

"Are you going to sea in it?"

"Yes."

"Come here, come to me, young Eve."

Clutching the skiff in my arms, I went to her over the clinking shingle and knelt down in front of her. She touched my face with her filthy, scabbed fingers. Her nails, dead matter, drily scratched my skin; she touched my eyes and my nose and my mouth as if she were reading them with her fingers. She exuded a rich smell of decay; her flesh had the substance of grave-clothes. She whisked away the blanket that covered me and touched my breasts and belly. Harsh, scabbed and rough as her hands were, her touch was as gentle as a surgeon's. She caught at my little pendant and fondled it, tugging it on its chain.

"Give me this, give me your necklace in return for my boat."

I unfastened the ingot of alchemical gold and gave it to her. She sniffed it, licked it, mumbled it, weighed it in her hand and seemed well pleased with it. She slipped it into the top half of her bikini, between her sunken dugs on which scattered drops of vodka caught the light from the air-raids and gleamed like pearlets of milk. She leaned back in her creaking, wicker chair and sighed, an old woman with hair